No one writes romantic fiction like Barbara Cartland.

Miss Cartland was originally inspired by the best of the romantic novelists she read as a girl—writers such as Elinor Glyn, Ethel M. Dell and E. M. Hull. Convinced that her own wide audience would also delight in her favorite authors, Barbara Cartland has taken their classic tales of romance and specially adapted them for today's readers.

Bantam is proud to publish these novels—personally selected and edited by Miss Cartland—under the imprint

BARBARA CARTLAND'S
LIBRARY OF LOVE

Bantam Books by Barbara Cartland
Ask your bookseller for the books you have missed

Barbara Cartland's Library of Love

Books of Love and Revelation

Other books by Barbara Cartland

The Obstacle Race

Ethel M. Dell

Condensed by Barbara Cartland

BANTAM BOOKS
TORONTO · NEW YORK · LONDON

THE OBSTACLE RACE
A Bantam Book / August 1980

ISBN 0-553-13912-6

Published simultaneously in the United States and Canada

Bantam Books are published by Bantam Books, Inc. Its trade-
mark, consisting of the words "Bantam Books" and the por-
trayal of a bantam, is Registered in U.S. Patent and Trademark
Office and in other countries. Marca Registrada. Bantam
Books, Inc., 666 Fifth Avenue, New York, New York 10103.

PRINTED IN THE UNITED STATES OF AMERICA

0 9 8 7 6 5 4 3 2 1

Introduction
by
Barbara Cartland

This dramatic, soul-disturbing story by Ethel M. Dell is gripping from the first page to the last. It is a struggle for all that is fine and noble in life against all that is frivolous and bad.

I think that when you have read *The Obstacle Race* you will feel, at the end, you have more courage to face the obstacles which all of us have in our own lives.

Chapter
One

A long green wave ran up, gleaming like curved glass in the sunlight, and broke in a million sparkles against a shelf of shingle.

"Columbus," said the girl, "this is just the place for us."

Columbus wagged a cheery tail and expressed complete agreement. He was watching a small crab hurrying among the stones. Suddenly the scuttling crab disappeared and he started up with a whine.

In a moment he was scratching in the shingle in eager search, flinging showers of stones over his companion in the process.

She protested, seizing him by his wiry tail to make him desist.

"Columbus! Don't! You're burying me alive! Do sit down and be sensible!"

Columbus subsided, not very willingly, dropping with a grunt into the hole he had made.

"The simple life doesn't include luxuries, Columbus!" she mused.

Her eyes looked out over the empty, tumbling sea, grey eyes, very level in their regard, under black brows that were absolutely straight.

She went on reflectively:

"I shall have to take in washing to eke out a modest living in chocolates. I wonder if there's a pawn-shop anywhere near."

Her voice was low and peculiarly soft, and she

uttered her words with something of a drawl. Her hands
were clasped about her knees, delicate hands that yet
looked capable.

"If I were Lady Joanna Farringmore, I suppose I
should say something rather naughty in French, Columbus, to relieve my feelings. But you and I don't talk
French, do we?"

She sighed.

"And we have struck the worthy Lady Jo and all her
crowd off our visiting-list for some time to come. I don't
suppose any of them will miss us much, do you, old
chap?"

She stretched out her arms suddenly towards the
horizon, then turned and lay down by Columbus on the
shingle.

"Oh, I'm glad we've cut adrift, aren't you?"

Again Columbus signified his agreement, after which,
as she seemed to have nothing further to say, he got up,
shook himself, and trotted off to explore the crannies in
the cliffs.

His mistress pillowed her dark head on her arm, and
lay still, with the sea singing along the ridge of shingle
below her. A brisk wind was blowing from the shore, but
the beach itself was sheltered.

The sunlight poured over her in a warm flood. It was
a perfect day in May.

Suddenly a small stone from nowhere fell with a
smart tap upon her uncovered head! She started, suprised
into full consciousness, and looked round.

The shore stretched empty behind her. There was no
sign of life among the grass-grown cliffs, save where
Columbus, some little distance away, was digging indus-
triously at the root of a small bush.

She searched the fringe of flaming gorse that over-
hung the top of the cliff immediately behind her, but
quite in vain. She gave up the search and lay down again.
Perhaps the wind had done it, though it did not seem very
likely.

The tide was rising and she would have to move soon
in any case. She would enjoy another ten minutes of her
delicious sun-bath before she returned for the midday
meal that Mrs. Rickett was preparing in the little cottage
next to the forge.

Again she stretched herself luxuriously. Yes, it was better than London. Again, reverie merged into drowsy absence of thought.

It fell upon her cheek this time with a sharp sting and bounced off onto her hand, a round black stone dropped from nowhere, but with strangely accurate aim.

She sprang up abruptly. This was getting beyond a joke.

Columbus was still routing beneath the distant bush. Most certainly he was not the offender. Some boy was hiding somewhere among the humps and clefts that constituted the rough surface of the cliff.

She picked up her walking-stick with a certain tightening of the lips. She would teach that boy a lesson if she caught him.

Grimly she set her face to the cliff and to the narrow, winding passage by which she had descended to the shore.

She sent forth a shrill whistle to Columbus as she began to climb the slippery path of stones. She was convinced that it was from this that her assailant had gathered his weapons.

And in a moment, turning inwards from the sea, she caught sight of a movement among some straggling bushes a few yards to one side of the path.

And then just as she reached the level, she stopped. It was as if a hand had caught her back. For suddenly there rose up before her a figure so strange that for a moment she felt almost like a scared child.

It sprang from the bushes and stood facing her like an animal at bay, a short creature neither man nor boy, misshapen, grotesquely humped.

The head was flung back and the face upraised, and it was the face that made her pause, for it was the most pathetic sight she had ever looked upon.

It was the face of a lad of twenty-two or -three, but drawn in lines so painful, so hollowed, so piteous, that fear melted into compassion at the sight. The dark eyes that stared upwards had a frightened look mingled with a certain defiance.

He stood barefooted on the edge of the cliff, clenching and unclenching his bony hands with the air of a culprit awaiting sentence.

After a moment she spoke, with as much sternness as she could muster.

"Why did you throw those stones?"

He backed at the sound of her voice, and she had an instant of sickening fear, for there was a drop of twenty feet behind him down to the shingle.

"Don't stand there!" she said quickly. "I'm not going to hurt you."

He lowered his head and looked at her from under drawn brows.

"Yes, you are," he said gruffly. "You're going to beat me with that stick."

. The shrewdness of this surmise struck her as not without humour. She smiled and, turning, flung the stick straight down to the path below.

"Now!" she said.

He came forward, not very willingly, and stood within a couple of yards of her, still looking as if he expected some sort of chastisement.

She faced him, and the last of her fear departed. Though he was so terribly deformed there was that about the face, sullen though it was, that stirred her deepest feelings.

She did her best to conceal the fact, however.

"Tell me why you threw those stones," she said.

"Because I wanted to hit you," he returned with disconcerting promptitude.

She looked at him steadily.

"How very unkind of you," she said.

His eyes gleamed with a smouldering resentment.

"No, it wasn't. I didn't want you there. Dicky is coming soon, and he likes it best when there is no-one there."

She noticed that though there was scant courtesy in his speech, it was by no means the rough talk of the fisherfolk. It fired her curiosity.

"And who is Dicky?" she asked.

"He's my brother. He knows heaps of things. He's a man."

"You are fond of him," said Juliet, with her friendly smile.

The boy's face lit up.

"He's the only person I love in the world," he replied, "except Mrs. Rickett's baby."

"I am staying with Mrs. Rickett," she said, "but I only came yesterday and I haven't made the baby's acquaintance yet. I must get myself introduced. You haven't told me your name yet. Mine is Juliet Moore."

He looked at her with renewed suspicion and asked:

"Hasn't anybody told you about me?"

"No, of course not. Why, I don't know anybody except Mr. and Mrs. Rickett. And it's much more interesting to hear it from yourself."

"Is it?" He hesitated a little longer, but was finally disarmed by the kindness of her smile. "My name is Robin."

"Oh, that's a nice name," Juliet said. "And you live here! What do you do all day?"

"I can mend fishing-nets, and I can help Dicky in the garden. And I look after Mrs. Rickett's baby sometimes when she's busy. What do you do?"

She made a slight gesture with her hands.

"Nothing at all worth doing, I'm afraid. I can't mend nets. I don't garden. And I've never looked after a baby in my life."

He stared at her.

"Where do you come from?" he asked curiously.

"From London."

She met his curiosity with absolute candour.

"And I'm tired of it. So I've come here for a change. I'm going to like this much better."

"Better than London!" He gazed, incredulous.

"Oh, much better."

Juliet spoke with absolute confidence.

"Ah, here is Columbus! He likes it better too."

She turned to greet her companion, who now came hastening up to view the new acquaintance.

He sniffed round Robin, who bent awkwardly and laid a fondling hand upon him.

"I like your dog," he said.

"That's right," said Juliet kindly. "We are both staying at the Ricketts', so when you come to see the baby, I hope you will come to see us, too. I must go now, or I shall be late for lunch. Good-bye!"

He shuffled his bare feet in the grass in embarrassment and murmured something she could not hear.

"What is it?" she said encouragingly, as if she were addressing a shy child.

He lifted his dark eyes to hers in sudden appeal.

"I say," he said with obvious effort, "if—if you meet Dicky, you—you won't tell him about—about . . ."

She checked the struggling words with a kindly gesture.

"Oh no, of course not! I'm not that sort of person. But the next time you want to get rid of me, just come and tell me so, and I'll go away at once!"

The gentleness of her words, uttered in that soft, slow voice of hers, had a curious effect upon her hearer. To her surprise, his eyes filled with tears.

"I shan't want to get rid of you! You're kind! I like you!" he blurted out.

"Oh, thank you very much!" Juliet replied, feeling oddly moved herself. "In that case, we are friends. Goodbye Come and see me soon!"

She smiled at him and departed, picking up her stick from the path and turning to wave to him as she continued the ascent.

From the top of the cliff she looked back and saw that he was still standing outlined against the shining sea behind him.

"Poor boy!" she murmured compassionately. "Poor ruined child! Columbus, we must be kind to him."

Columbus looked up with knowing eyes and wagged his tail. He had taken to the lad himself.

*　　*　　*

"Lor' bless you!" said Mrs. Rickett. "There's some folks as thinks young Robin is the plague of the neighbourhood, but there ain't no harm in the lad if he's let alone."

She shook her head in despair.

"It's when them little varmints of village boys sets on him and teases him as he ain't safe.

"Why, I've seen him go away into a corner and cry like a baby at a sharp word from his brother Dick. He sets such store by him."

"Was he born like that?" asked Juliet, as her inform-ant paused for breath.

Mrs. Rickett pursed her lips.

"Well, you see, Miss, he were a twin, and he never did thrive from the very earliest. But he wasn't a hunch-back, not like he is now, at first."

She paused, then continued:

"The poor mother died when they were born. She was a lady born and bred, but married beneath her. She didn't have any such life of it either. He were a Sea Captain, a funny fellow with a frightful temper."

Her face wore an expression of contempt as she continued:

"He never come home for twelve years after Dick were born. She used to teach at the village school. Very sweet in her ways she were. Everyone liked her. There's them as says Mr. Fielding was in love with her. He didn't marry, you know, till long after."

Her voice deepened before she went on:

"And then, quite sudden-like, when everyone thought he'd been dead for years, her husband come home again. He was a beast, and he hadn't improved in them twelve years. He were a hard drinker, and he used to torment her to drink with him; used to knock young Dick about too, something cruel."

She shuddered.

"I'll never forget the change in her, never as long as I live. Her spirit was quite broke, and when the babies come she hadn't a chance. It happened very quick at the last, and her husband weren't there. She only asked for Dick, and he was with her just at the end."

She sighed.

"He was only a lad of thirteen, Miss, but from that night on he was a man grown. She begged him to look after the babies, and he promised her he would.

"Then she just lay holding his hand till she died. No-one ever saw young Dick break down after that. He's got a will like steel."

"And the horrible husband?" Juliet asked, now thor-oughly interested in Mrs. Rickett's tragedy.

"I were coming to him," said Mrs. Rickett, with obvious relish. "He was at The Three Tuns till closing-time, then he went out roaring drunk, and went over the cliff in the dark. The tide was up and he was drowned. A great pity it didn't happen a little bit sooner, says I!"

She shook her head.

"Believe me, Miss, there's no martyrdom so bad as getting married to the wrong man. I've seen it once and again, and I knows."

"I quite agree with you," said Juliet. "But tell me some more! Who took care of the poor babies?"

"Mrs. Cross at the lodge took them. Mr. Fielding, the Squire, provided for 'em, and he helped young Dick along, too. He's been very good to them. He had young Jack trained, and now he's his Chauffeur. But he's wild. Dick often finds him a handful.

"Robin can't abide him, which isn't to be wondered at, seeing as it was mostly Jack's fault that he's a cripple!"

"Why?" Juliet asked.

"Jack led him into all sorts of mischief, till one day when they were about ten they went off birds'-nesting along the cliffs, and only Jack come back late at night to say his brother had gone over the cliff."

She paused, then continued:

"Dick tore off with some of the chaps from the shore. It were dark and windy, and they all said it was no use, but Dick insisted upon going down the face of the cliff on a rope to find him. And find him at last he did, on a ledge about a hundred feet down."

"How awful!" Juliet exclaimed.

"He was so badly hurt that he thought he'd broke his back, and he didn't dare move him till morning, but just stayed there with him all night long. Oh, it was a dreadful business."

A large tear splashed unchecked onto Mrs. Rickett's apron.

"Robin was on his back for nearly a year after, and then, when he began to get about again, them humps came and he grew crooked!"

Her voice broke as she went on:

"Dick were reading for the law, but he gave it all up and turned Schoolmaster, so as he could live here and take care of young Robin."

"Turned Schoolmaster!" Juliet repeated the words. "He's something of a scholar, then!"

"No, no," said Mrs. Rickett. "It's only the village school, Miss. Mr. Fielding got him the post. They're an unruly set of varmints here, but he keeps order among 'em."

She smiled as she said:

"He does his best to civilise 'em, and all them fisher-chaps thinks a deal of him too. They've got a club at the village what Mr. Fielding built for 'em, and Dick goes along there and gives 'em musical evenings and jollies 'em generally.

"The mines belongs to the Farringmore family, you know, Lord Wilchester owns 'em. But he never comes near, and o' course the men gets discontented and difficult.

"But Dick can always handle 'em, knows 'em inside and out, and their wives too. Yes, he's very clever is Dick. But he's thrown away in this place.

"It's a pity, you know. If it weren't for Robin, it's my belief that he'd be a great man. He's a born leader. But he's never had a chance, and it don't look like as if he ever will now, poor fellow!"

"How old is he?" asked Juliet.

"Oh, he's a lot past thirty now, getting too old to turn his hand to anything new. Mr. Fielding, he's always on to him about it, but it don't make no difference.

"He'll never take up any other work while Robin lives. And Robin is stronger than he used to be, all thanks to Dick's care. He's just sacrificed everything to that boy, you know. It don't seem hardly right, do it?"

"I don't know," Juliet said slowly. "Some sacrifices are worthwhile."

* * *

The scent of the gorse in the evening dew was as incense offered to the stars. To Juliet, wandering forth in the twilight after supper, with Columbus, the exquisite fragrance was almost intoxicating.

The sea was like a dream-sea also, silver under the stars, barely rippling against the shingle, immensely and mysteriously calm. She went on and on, scarcely feeling the ground beneath her feet, moving through an atmosphere of pure magic.

Suddenly, from somewhere not far distant among the gorse bushes, there came a sound. She stopped, and it seemed to her that all the world stopped with her to hear the first soft trill of a nightingale through the tender dusk.

Then Columbus came careering along the path in fevered search of her; and quite suddenly, like the closing of a lid, the magic sounds vanished into a deep silence.

"Oh, Columbus!" his mistress murmured reproachfully. "You've stopped the music!"

She yielded to his persuasion, and walked on up the path, with her face to the shimmering sea. For some reason she felt divinely happy.

It was almost at the same moment that there came from behind her a sound that shattered all the fairy romance of the night at a blow.

She turned sharply, and immediately, like a fiendish chorus, it came again, spreading and echoing along the cliffs—the yelling of drunken laughter.

Several men were coming along the path that she had travelled. She saw them vaguely in the dimness a little way below her, and realised that her retreat in that direction was cut off.

They came up the path, yelling like hounds on a scent, while she stood perfectly erect and motionless, facing them. There were five of them, hulking youths all inflamed by drink.

She stood her ground with her back to the cliff edge, not yielding an inch, contempt in every line.

"Will you kindly go your way," she said, "and allow me to go mine?"

They responded with yells of derision, and one young man, emboldened by the jeers of his companions, came close to her and leered into her face of rigid disdain.

"I am damned if I won't have a kiss first!" he swore, and flung a rough arm about her.

Juliet moved with the fierce suddenness of a wild thing trapped. She wrenched herself from him in furious disgust.

"You hound!" she began to say.

But the word was never fully uttered, for as it sprang to her lips it went into a desperate cry.

The ground had given way beneath her feet, and she fell straight backwards over that awful edge.

For the fraction of an instant she saw the stars in the deep-blue sky above her, then, like the snap of a spring, they vanished into darkness. . . .

It was a darkness that spread and spread like an endless sea, submerging all things. No light could penetrate it; only a few vague sounds and impressions somehow filtered through.

And then she was aware of someone lifting her out of the depth that had received her.

She came to herself gasping, but for some reason she dared not look up. That single glimpse of the wheeling universe seemed to have sealed her vision.

Then a voice spoke:

"I say, do open your eyes, if you don't mind! You're not really dead. You've only had a tumble."

That voice awakened her quite effectually. The mixture of entreaty and common sense it contained strangely stirred her curiosity. She opened her eyes wide upon the speaker.

"Hullo!" she said faintly.

He was kneeling by her side, looking closely into her face, and the first thing that struck her was the extreme brightness of his eyes. They shone like black onyx.

He responded at once, his voice very low and rapid:

"It's perfectly all right. You needn't be afraid. I was just in time to catch you. Feeling better now? Like to sit up?"

She awoke to the fact that she was propped against his knee. She sat up, still gasping a little, but shrank as she realised the narrowness of the ledge on which she rested.

He thrust out a protecting arm in front of her.

"It's all right. You're absolutely safe. You couldn't go over if you tried. Don't look if it makes you giddy!"

She looked again into his face, and again was struck by the amazing keenness of his eyes.

"How did you get here?" she asked.

"It's easy enough when you know the way. I was just coming to help you when you came over. You didn't hear me shout?"

"No. They were all making such a horrid noise." She suppressed a shudder. "Have they gone now?"

"Yes, the brutes! They scooted. I'm going after them directly."

"Oh, please don't!" she said hastily. "Not for the world! I don't want to be left alone here. I've had enough of it."

She tried to smile with the words, but it was rather a trembling attempt. He abandoned his intention at once.

"All right. It'll keep. Look here, shall I help you up? You'll feel better on the top."

"I think I had better stay here for a minute," Juliet said. "I . . . I'm afraid I shall make an idiot of myself if I don't."

"No, you won't. You'll be all right."

He thrust an abrupt arm round her shoulders, gripping them hard to still her trembling.

"Lean against me! I've got you quite safe."

She relaxed with a murmur of thanks. There was something intensely reassuring about that firm grip. She sat quite motionless for a space, gradually regaining her self-command.

In the end, a snuffle and whine from above aroused her. She sat up with a start.

"Oh, Columbus! Don't let him fall over!"

Her companion laughed a little.

"Let's go back to him then! Don't look down! Keep your face to the cliff! And remember, I've got hold of you, so you can't fall."

She struggled blindly to her feet, helped by his arm behind her; but she was seized immediately by an overwhelming giddiness that made her totter back against him.

"I'm dreadfully sorry," she said, almost in tears. "I can't help it. I'm an idiot."

He held her up with unfailing steadiness.

"All right!" he replied. "Don't get frightened! Move along slowly with me!"

She came to a standstill, clinging desperately to the unyielding stone.

"I can't possibly do it," she answered helplessly.

"Yes, you can. You've got to."

He loosened her clutching fingers with the words, and pushed her onwards. She went, driven by a force such as she had never encountered before.

She heard the soft wash of the sea far below her, above the sickening thudding of her heart, as she crept forward round that terrible bend.

She was aware of a very firm hand that grasped her shoulder, impelling her forward. There was no resisting that steady pressure.

She came to the steps. The path had widened somewhat, and the dreadful sense of sheer depth below her was less insistent. Nevertheless, the way was far from easy, the steps being little more than deep notches in the cliff.

Her guide came immediately behind her. She felt his hand touch her at every step she took. Just at the last, realising the nearness of the summit and safety, she tried to hurry, and in a moment slipped.

He grabbed her instantly, but she could not recover her footing though she made a frantic effort to do so.

She sprawled against the cliff, clutching madly at some tufts of grass and weed above her, while the man behind her gripped and held her there.

He put forth his full strength then. She felt the strain of his muscles as he gathered her up with one arm. He drew a deep hard breath, and began to climb.

It was only a few feet to the top, as he had said, but the climb seemed to her unending. She was conscious throughout that his endurance was being put to the utmost test.

But he never faltered, and finally, just when she had begun to wonder if this awful nightmare of danger could never cease, she found herself set down upon the dewy grass that covered the top of the cliff.

The scent of the gorse bushes came again to her and the far sweet call of the nightingale. She saw again the shimmering, wonderful sea and the ever-brightening stars.

Then Columbus came pushing and nuzzling against her, and something that she did not fully understand made her turn and clasp him closely, with a sudden rush of tears.

The danger was over, all over. And never till this moment had she realised how amazingly sweet was life.

＊　＊　＊

She laughed very shakily at the solicitude expressed by Columbus, and told him tremulously how absurd and ridiculous he was to make such a fuss about nothing.

After this, feeling a little better, she ventured a glance at her companion. He was a man of medium height and no great breadth of shoulder, but evidently well-knit and athletic.

She saw his eyes gleam under black, mobile brows that seemed to denote a considerable sense of humour. The whole of his face held an astonishing amount of vitality, but the lips were straight and rather hard.

He looked to her like a man who would suffer to the utmost but never lose his self-control. And she thought she read a pride more than ordinary in the case of his features.

Then he spoke, and curiously all criticism vanished.

"I had better introduce myself," he said. "I'm afraid I've been unpardonably rude. My name is Green."

Swiftly she rose to her feet and offered her hand to her cavalier.

"How do you do, Mr. Green? My name is Moore ... Miss Moore. Will you allow me to thank you for saving my life?"

Her voice throbbed a little; tears and laughter were equally near the surface at that moment.

"I say, please don't!" he said. "I wouldn't have missed it for anything. It was jolly plucky of you to stand your ground with those hooligans from the mine."

"But I didn't stand my ground," she pointed out. "I went over. It was a most undignified proceeding, wasn't it?"

"No, it wasn't," he declared. "You did it awfully well. I wish I'd been nearer to you, but I couldn't possibly get up in time."

"Oh, I think you were more useful where you were," she said, "thank you all the same. I would have gone clean to the bottom otherwise. I thought I had."

She caught back an involuntary shudder, and in a

moment the hand that held hers closed unceremoniously and drew her farther from the edge of the cliff.

"You are sure you are none the worse now?" he questioned. "Not giddy, or anything?"

"No, not anything," she replied.

But she was glad of his hold nonetheless, and he seemed to know it, for he kept her hand firmly clasped.

"You must let me see you back," he said. "Where are you staying?"

"At Mrs. Rickett's," she told him. "The village smithy, you know."

"I know," he said. "Down at Little Shale, you mean. You've come some way, haven't you?"

"It was such a lovely night," she sighed, "and Columbus wanted a walk. I got led on. I didn't know I was likely to meet anyone."

"It's the short-cut to High Shale," he explained. "There is always the chance of meeting these fellows along here. You'd be safer going the other way."

"But I like the furze bushes and the nightingales," she said regretfully, "and the exquisite wildness of it. It's not nearly so nice the other way."

He laughed.

"No, but it's safer. Come this way as much as you like in the morning, but go the other way at night!"

He turned with the words, and began to lead her down the path. She went with him as one who responds instinctively to a power unquestioned.

"This is the most wonderful place I have ever seen," she said at last in a tone of awe.

"Is it?"

His lack of enthusiasm surprised her.

"Don't you think so too?" she questioned. "Doesn't it seem wonderful to you?"

He glanced out to sea for a moment.

"You see, I live here. Yes, it's quite a beautiful place. But it isn't always like this. It's primitive. It can be savage. You wouldn't like it always."

"I'm thinking of settling down here, all the same," said Juliet.

He stopped short in the path.

"Are you really?"

She nodded, with a smile.

"You seem surprised. Why shouldn't I? Isn't there room for one more?"

"Oh, plenty of room," he stated, and walked on again as abruptly as he had paused.

The path became wider and more level, and he relinquished her hand.

"You won't stay," he said with conviction.

"I wonder," Juliet replied.

"Of course you won't!" A hint of vehemence crept into his speech. "When the nightingales have left off singing and the wild roses are over, you'll go."

"You seem very sure of that."

"Yes, I am sure."

He spoke uncompromisingly, almost contemptuously, she thought.

"You evidently don't stay here because you like it," she said.

"My work is here," he returned noncommittally.

She wondered a little, but something held her back from pursuing the matter.

"I wish I could find work here," she said in her slow, deep voice. "It would do me a lot of good."

"It depends upon what your capabilities are."

"My capabilities!" She laughed a soft, low laugh.

"My capabilities!" she mused. "Let me see. What can I do?"

She looked at her companion with a smile.

"I am afraid I shall have to refer you to Lady Joanna Farringmore. She can tell you exactly."

He made a slight movement of surprise.

"You know the Farringmore family?"

She raised her brows a little.

"Yes. Do you?"

"By hearsay only. Lord Wilchester owns the High Shale Mines. I have never met any of them." He spoke without enthusiasm.

"And never want to?" she suggested. "I quite understand. I am very tired of them myself just now . . . most especially of Lady Joanna. But perhaps it is rather bad taste to say so, as I have been brought up as her Companion from childhood."

"And now you have left her?" he questioned.

"Yes, I have left her. I have disapproved of her for some time." Juliet spoke thoughtfully. "She is very unconventional, you know. And I ... well, at heart I fancy I must be rather a prude. Anyhow, I disapproved, more and more strongly, and at last I came away."

"That was rather brave of you," he commented.

"Oh, it wasn't much of a sacrifice. I am going to cultivate a contented mind here. And when I go back to Lady Jo ... if I ever do ... I shall be proof against anything."

"I think you will probably go back long before the contented mind has begun to sprout."

She laughed as she walked on down the path.

"But it has begun already. I haven't felt so cheerful for a long time."

"That isn't real contentment," he pointed out. "It's your spirit of adventure enjoying itself. Wait till you begin to be bored!"

"I am not going to be bored. My spirit of adventure is not at all an enterprising one. I assure you I didn't enjoy that tumble over the cliff in the least. I am a very quiet person by nature."

She began to laugh.

"You must have noticed that I wasn't very intrepid in the face of danger. I seem to remember you telling me not to be silly."

"I hoped you had forgiven and forgotten that," he said.

"Neither one nor the other," she answered, checking her mirth. "I think you would have been absolutely justified in using even stronger language under the circumstances. You wouldn't have saved me if you hadn't been ... very firm."

"Very brutal, you mean. No, I ought to have managed better. I will next time."

He spoke with a smile, but there was a hint of seriousness in his words.

"When will that be?" asked Juliet.

"I don't know. But I can make the way down much easier. The steps are a simple matter, and I have often thought a charge of gunpowder would improve that bit where the rock hangs over. If I hadn't wanted to keep the place to myself I should have done it long ago. It certainly is dangerous now to anyone who doesn't know."

Juliet came to a sudden halt in the path.

"Oh, you are an engineer. I hope you will not spoil your favourite eyrie just because I may someday fall over into it again.

"Now, please don't come any farther with me! It has only just dawned on me that your way probably lies in the direction of the mines."

He looked momentarily surprised.

"But I do live in this direction. In any case, I hope you will allow me to see you safely back."

"But there is no need," she protested. "We are practically there. Do you really live this way?"

"Yes. Quite close to the worthy Mrs. Rickett too. I am not an engineer. I am the village Schoolmaster."

He announced the fact with absolute directness. It was Juliet's turn to look surprised. She almost gasped.

"You . . . you!"

"Yes, I. Why not?" He met her look of astonishment with a smile. "Have I given you a shock?"

She recovered herself with an answering smile.

"No, of course not. I might have guessed. I wonder I didn't."

"But how could you guess?" he questioned. "Have I the manners of a pedagogue?"

"No," she said again. "No, of course not. Only . . . I have been hearing a good deal about you today; not in your capacity of Schoolmaster, but as . . . Brother Dick."

"Ah!" he said sharply, and just for a moment she thought he was either embarrassed or annoyed, but whatever the feeling he covered it instantly. "You have talked to my brother Robin?"

"Yes. We met on the shore."

"I hope he behaved himself," he said. "You weren't afraid of him, I hope?"

"No, poor lad! Why should I be?" Juliet spoke very gently, very pityingly. "I have a feeling that Robin and I are going to be friends."

"You are very good," he said in a low voice. "He hasn't many friends, poor chap. But he's very faithful to those he's got."

They had reached the road that turned up to the village, and the light from a large lamp some distance up the hill shone down upon them.

"That is where Mr. Fielding lives," said Green, as they walked towards it. "Those are his lodge gates. No doubt you have heard of him too. He is the great man of the place. He owns it, in fact."

"Yes, I have heard of him," Juliet replied. "Is he a nice man?"

He made an almost imperceptible movement of the shoulders.

"I am very much indebted to him."

"I see."

They reached the cottage gate that led to the black-smith's humble abode. Juliet paused and held out her hand.

"Good-bye!" she said.

His grasp was strong and very steady.

"Good-bye! I hope you'll find what you're looking for."

The gate closed behind her, and Juliet walked up the path with Columbus trotting sedately by her side. She heard her escort's departing footsteps as she went, and wondered when they would meet again.

Chapter Two

The Church at Little Shale was very ancient and picturesque. It stood almost opposite the hedge gates of Shale Court, the abode of the great Mr. Fielding.

Juliet entered the Church, which smelt of the mould of centuries, and paused inside.

After a brief hesitation, she sat down in a chair close to the porch.

Footsteps came up the path, and on the very verge of the porch a voice spoke—a woman's voice, unmodulated, arrogant.

"Really, Edward! I don't see why your village School-master should be asked to lunch every Sunday."

The words were scarcely uttered before the notes of the organ swelled suddenly through the Church. Juliet felt an indignant flush rise in her cheeks.

She was certain that that remark had been audible all over the Church, and she resented it with vehemence.

Then with a sweep of feathers and laces the speaker entered, and Juliet raised her eyes to regard her.

She saw a young woman, delicate-looking, with a pretty, insolent face and expensive clothes, walk past, and was aware for a moment of a haughty stare that seemed to question her right to be there.

Then her own attention passed to the man who entered in a somewhat ordinary style, but he walked with the suggestion of a swagger, as if ready to challenge any who should dispute his right to the place and everyone in it.

His wife entered the great square pew, but he strode on to the chancel, tapped the Organist unceremoniously on the shoulder, and spoke to him.

Juliet watched the result with a curiosity she could not restrain. The black head turned sharply. She caught a momentary glimpse of Green's energetic profile as he spoke briefly and emphatically.

The Squire marched back to his pew, still frowning, and the voluntary continued. He played with assurance, but somewhat mechanically, and presently she realised that he was keeping a sharp eye on the schoolchildren at the same time.

The service was a lengthy one, and they needed supervision. It was certainly a hot morning, and the sermon very dull.

When it was over at last she was the first to leave the Church, and wandering down the path through the hot, chequered sunlight she saw the shining car drawn up at the gate, and a young Chauffeur waiting at the door.

She glanced at him as she passed, and was surprised for a second to find him gazing at her with a curious intentness. He lowered his eyes the moment they met hers, and she passed on, wondering what there was about her to excite his interest.

Columbus was waiting with pathetic patience to be taken for a walk, and, overpoweringly hot though it was, she had not the heart to keep him any longer.

But she could not face the full blaze of the noon on the shore, and she turned back up the shady Church-lane with a vague memory of having seen a stile at the entrance of a wood somewhere along its winding length.

The green glades of the wood received her; she wandered forward with a delightful sense of well-being. She sat down on a mossy root and drank in the sweetness with a deep content.

Columbus was busy trying to unearth a wood-louse that had eluded him in a tuft of grass. She watched him lazily.

He persevered for a long time, in fact till the tuft of grass was practically demolished, and then at last, failing in his quest, he relinquished the search and with a deep sigh lay down by her side.

Juliet looked up. Someone was coming along the

winding path through the wood. The next moment a figure came in sight, and she recognised the Squire.

He was walking quickly, impatiently flicking a stick to and fro as he came. The frown still drew his forehead, and she saw at the first glance that he was annoyed.

He did not see her at first, in fact not until he was close upon her. Then, as Columbus tactlessly repeated his growl, he started and his look fell upon her.

Juliet had had no intention of speaking, but his eyes held so direct a question that she was found herself compelled to do so.

"I hope we are not trespassing," she said.

He put his hand to his hat with a jerk.

"You are not, Madam," he replied. "I am not so sure of the dog."

His voice was not unpleasant, but no smile accompanied his words. At close quarters she saw that he was older than she had at first believed him to be. He was well on in the fifties.

She drew Columbus nearer to her.

"I won't let him hunt," she said.

"He will probably get shot if he does," remarked Mr. Fielding, and was gone without further ceremony.

Mrs. Rickett's midday meal was fixed for half-past-one. She was not looking forward to it with any great relish, but not for worlds would she have had the good woman know it.

She got up and began to walk back. But, nearing the stile, the sound of voices made her pause. Two men were evidently standing there, and she realised with something like dismay that the way was blocked.

She waited for a moment or two, then decided to put a bold face on it and pursue her course. Mrs. Rickett's dinner certainly would not improve by keeping.

She pressed on, therefore, and, as she drew nearer, she recognised the Squire's voice, raised on a note of irritation.

"Oh, don't be a fool, my good fellow! I shouldn't ask you if I didn't really want you."

The answer came instantly, and though it sounded curt it had a ring of humour.

"Thank you, Sir. And I shouldn't refuse if I really wanted to come."

It was at this point that Juliet rounded a curve in the path and came within sight of the stile.

Mr. Green was standing facing her, and she saw his instant glance of recognition. Mr. Fielding had his back to her, and the younger man laid a hand upon his arm and drew him aside.

Mr. Fielding turned sharply. He looked her up and down with a resentful stare as she mounted the stile, and Juliet flushed in spite of her most determined composure.

Mr. Green came forward instantly and offered a hand to assist her.

"Good-morning, Miss Moore! Exploring in another direction today?"

She took the proffered hand, feeling absurdly embarrassed by the Squire's presence.

Mr. Green was bareheaded and his hair shone in the strong sunlight. His manner was absolutely easy and assured. She met his smiling look with an odd feeling of gratitude, as if he had ranged himself on her side against something formidable.

"I am afraid I haven't been very fortunate in my choice today either," she said somewhat ruefully, as she descended.

He laughed.

"We all trespass in these woods. It's a time-honoured custom, isn't it, Mr. Fielding? The pheasants are quite used to it."

Juliet did not glance in the Squire's direction. She felt that she had done all that was necessary in that quarter and that any further overture would but meet with a churlish response.

But to her astonishment he took the initiative.

"I am afraid I wasn't too hospitable just now. It's the fellow's fault, Dick, it's up to you to apologise on my behalf."

Juliet looked at him then in amazement, and saw that he was actually smiling at her, such a smile as transformed him completely.

"If Miss Moore will permit me," said Mr. Green, with a bow, "I will introduce you to her. You will then be *en rapport* and in a position to apologise for yourself."

"Pedagogue!" said the Squire.

And Juliet laughed for the first time.

"If anyone apologises it should be I," she replied.

She smiled at the Squire.

"Good-bye! I must be getting back to Mrs. Rickett's or the dumplings will be cold."

She whistled Columbus to her and departed, still wondering at the transformation which Mr. Green had wrought in the Squire.

* * *

"May I come and see you?" asked Robin.

Juliet, seated under an apple tree in the tiny orchard that stood beside the road, looked up from her book and saw his thin face peering at her through the hedge.

"Of course!" she replied. "I am very pleased to see you."

But he still stood, glowering at her uncertainly near the hedge.

"Come along, then!" said Juliet kindly.

She smiled down at him.

"You are going to stay and have tea with me, aren't you?"

He smiled rather doubtfully in answer.

"I'd like to. I don't know if I can, though."

"Why shouldn't you?" she questioned.

He folded his long arms about his knees and murmured something unintelligible.

Juliet moved impulsively and laid her hand upon his humped shoulder. He rested his chin upon her hand, looking up at her dumbly. Her heart stirred within her. The pathos of those eyes was more than she could meet unmoved.

He edged himself nearer to her.

"I like you," he said. "Talk to me! I like your voice."

"What shall I talk about?"

"Tell me about London!"

"Oh, London! You'd hate London. It's all noise and crowds and dust. The streets are crammed with cars and people, and there is never any peace."

Robin was listening with deep interest.

"Is that why you came here?" he questioned.

"Yes. I was tired out and rather scared. I got away just in time . . . only just in time."

His eyes sought hers again.

"You're not frightened, then, any more?"

She smiled at him.

"No, not a bit. I've got over that, and I'm beginning to enjoy myself."

"Shall you stay here always?"

"I don't know, Robin. I'm not going to look ahead. I'm just going to make the best of the present. Don't you think that's the best way?"

He made a wry face.

"I suppose it is—if you don't know what's coming."

"But no-one knows that," replied Juliet.

He glanced at her. His fingers, clasped about his knees, tugged restlessly at one another.

"I know what's going to happen to me," he said after a moment. "I'm going to get into a row—with Dicky."

Her heart went out to him, he looked so forlorn.

"Why don't you go and tell him you're sorry?" she said gently.

"Not sorry," articulated Robin, with a sniff.

The matter presented difficulties. Juliet tried to hedge.

"What have you been doing?"

"Quarrelling," replied Robin.

"What! With Dick?"

"No!" Again he glanced at her, and wiped a hasty hand across his eyes. "Dick!" he repeated, as if in derision at her colossal ignorance.

"Well, but who, then?" she questioned.

"It was—Jack." He suddenly turned to her fully with blazing eyes.

"I hate Jack!" he said very emphatically.

"Jack! But who is Jack? Oh, I remember!" Juliet abruptly recalled the young Chauffeur at the Church-yard gate. "He is your other brother, isn't he? I'd forgotten him."

"He's a—beast!" said Robin. "I hate him."

His look challenged reproof. Juliet wisely made none.

"Isn't he kind to you?" she asked.

"It wasn't that!" blurted out Robin. "It—it—was what he said about—about . . ."

He suddenly stopped, closed his lips, and sat savagely biting them.

"About what?" questioned Juliet, bewildered.

Robin sat mute.

"I should forget it if I were you," she said sensibly. "People often do and say things they don't mean. It doesn't pay to be too sensitive. Let's forget it, shall we?"

"I can't. Dicky's angry."

He paused, then continued with an effort:

"He said I wasn't to come here, said—said he'd punish me if I did. He called me back, and I wouldn't go. He . . ."

He suddenly broke off.

"He's coming now!" he whispered.

The gate had clicked, and Columbus, who had accepted Robin without question, bustled forward to investigate.

Robin pressed closer to Juliet. She could feel him trembling. Instinctively she laid her hand upon him as his brother drew near.

"Have you come to see me or to look for Robin?" she asked.

Mr. Green's look was enigmatical. It comprehended them both at a single glance. She wondered if he was really angry, but, if so, he had himself under complete control.

"Mr. Green, please, don't . . . be angry with Robin!"

His look flashed straight down to her. His eyes were still smiling, yet very strangely they compelled her own.

He stooped unexpectedly after an instant's pause, lifted her hand with absolute gentleness away from Robin, and laid it in her lap.

"Get up!" he commanded. "And don't be an ass!"

There was no questioning the kindess of his voice. Robin lifted his head, stared a moment, then blundered to his feet.

"He is staying to tea with me," said Juliet.

"Oh, I think not," Mr. Green replied. "Another time —if you are kind enough. Not today."

He spoke very decidedly. Robin, with his head hanging, turned away.

Mr. Green, with a brief gesture of farewell, turned to follow. But in that moment Juliet spoke in that full rich voice of hers that was all the more arresting because she did not raise it.

"Mr. Green, I want to speak to you."

He stopped at once. She thought she caught a glint of humour behind the courteous attention of his eyes.

"Forgive me for interfering!" she said. "But I must say it."

She looked up at him doubtfully for a moment or two. Then hesitatingly, she spoke.

"Please . . . don't . . . punish Robin for coming here!"

She saw his brows go up in surprise. He was about to speak, but she went on with more than a touch of embarrassment:

"Perhaps it sounds impertinent, but I believe I could help him in some ways . . . if I had the chance. Anyhow, I should like to try. Please let him come and see me as often as he likes."

"Really?" said Mr. Green, and stopped. The amusement had wholly gone out of his look.

"I don't know what to say to you," he said in a moment. "You are so awfully kind."

Juliet's smile was oddly wistful.

"I assure you I am selfish to the core. But there's something about Robin that goes straight to my heart. I should like to be kind to him . . . for my own sake. So don't . . . please . . . try to keep him out of my way!"

She spoke very earnestly, her eyes under their straight brows looking directly into his honest eyes that no man could doubt.

Mr. Green stood facing her, his look as kind as her own.

"Do you know, Miss Moore, I think this is about the kindest thing that has ever come into my experience?"

She made a slight gesture of protest.

"Oh, but don't let us talk in superlatives. Fetch Robin back, and both of you stay to tea!"

He shook his head.

"Not today. I am very sorry. But he doesn't deserve it. He has been getting a bit out-of-hand lately. I can't pass it over."

Juliet leant forward in her chair. Her eyes were suddenly very bright.

"This once, Mr. Green!"

He stiffened a little.

"No!"

"You won't?"

"I can't."

Juliet's look went beyond him to the figure of Robin leaning disconsolately against a distant tree. She sat for several moments watching him, while Mr. Green stood before her as if waiting to be dismissed.

"Poor boy!" she said softly, at length, and turned again to the man in front of her. "Are you sure you understand him?"

"Yes."

"And you are not hard on him? You are never hard on him?"

"He came here in direct defiance of my orders."

"I know. He told me. Please never give him such orders again!"

"You are awfully kind. But really in this case there was sufficient reason. Some people—most people—prefer him at a distance."

"I am not one of them," Juliet replied.

"I see you are not. But I couldn't risk it. Besides, he was in a towering rage when he started. It isn't fair to inflict him on people in that state."

"I should never be afraid of him," Juliet said quietly. "I think I know . . . partly . . . what was the matter. Someone made a rather cruel remark about him, and someone else maliciously repeated it."

"I know," he said in a low voice. "It's hard for him, poor chap! As long as he lives, he's got to bear his burden."

"But it needn't be made heavier than it is," Juliet replied.

"No, it needn't. But it isn't everyone that sees it in that light. I'm glad you do, anyway, and I'm grateful—on Robin's behalf. Good-bye!"

He lifted his hand again in a farewell salute and turned away.

A few seconds later they passed her on the other side

of the hedge, evidently on their way to the shore, and she
heard Robin's voice as they went by.

"I'm sorry now, Dicky."

She turned her head to catch his brother's answer, for
it did not come immediately and she wondered a little at
the delay.

Then, as they drew farther away, she heard him
say:

"Why did you do that?"

"She told me to," replied Robin.

She felt her colour rise and heard Mr. Green laugh.
They were almost out of earshot before he said:

"All right, boy! I'll let you off this time. Don't do it
again."

She leant back in her chair and reopened her book.
But she did not read for some time. Somehow she felt
glad, quite unreasonably glad, that Robin had been let
off.

* * *

The evening light spread golden over the apple trees
in the orchard. Juliet was wandering among the falling
blossoms when she heard the sound of hoof-beats in the
lane.

A moment later the Squire came into view. He
fastened his animal to the porch and turned towards the
orchard.

"May I come through?" he enquired.

"Oh, pray do!" Juliet opened the gate with the words,
and held out her hand.

She was aware of his eyes looking at her very searchingly as he took her hand.

"I hope you don't mind a visitor at this hour?" he
asked.

She smiled.

"No. I am quite at liberty. Come and sit down!"

She led the way to a bench under the apple trees,
and the Squire tramped after her with jingling spurs.

"I'm afraid you'll think me very unconventional," he
said, speaking with a sort of arrogant humility as she
stopped.

"I like unconventional people best," Juliet answered.

He dropped down onto the seat.

"Oh, do you? Then I needn't apologise any further. You've been here about a week, haven't you?"

"Yes."

"You came from London?"

"Yes," she said again.

He began to frown and to pull restlessly at the lash of his riding-whip.

"Do you think me impertinent for asking you questions?" he asked.

"Not so far," said Juliet.

He uttered a brief laugh.

"You're cautious. Listen, Miss Moore. What I really came to ask is—do you want a job?"

Juliet stiffened a little.

"What sort of a job?"

His fingers tugged more and more vigorously at the leather. She realised quite suddenly that he was embarrassed, and at once her own embarrassment passed.

"Have you come to offer me a job?" she said. "How kind of you to think of it!"

"It was on Sunday," said Fielding. "My wife saw you in Church. She took rather a fancy to you.

"Well, after Green's introduction, when you had gone, I asked him if he knew anything about you. He said he had only made your acquaintance the day before, and that you had told him that you had held the post of Companion to someone, he didn't say who."

He paused, then went on:

"And I wondered if possibly you might feel inclined to see how you got on with my wife in that capacity. She is not strong. She wants a Companion."

Juliet's grey eyes gazed steadily before her as she listened.

As he ended she turned towards him, still caressing the dog at her feet.

"Wouldn't it be better," she said, "if Mrs. Fielding knew me before offering me such a post?"

The Squire smiled at her abruptly.

"No, I don't think so. It wouldn't be worthwhile unless you mean to consider it."

It was Juliet's turn to smile.

"But I can't possibly decide until we have met, can I?"

"Does that mean you'll consider it?" asked the Squire.

"I am considering it," said Juliet. "But please give me time! For I have only just begun."

"That's fair," he conceded. "How long will it take you?"

She began to laugh.

"You haven't told me any details yet."

"Well, what do you want to know? My wife always breakfasts in bed, so she wouldn't want you before ten. But you'd live with us, of course. I'd see that they made you comfortable."

"If my duties did not begin before ten, there would be no need for that," pointed out Juliet.

He looked at her in surprise.

"Of course you'd live with us! You can't want to stay here!"

"But why not?" asked Juliet. "They are very kind to me. I am very happy here. But go on, if you don't mind! What happens after ten o'clock?"

"Well, she opens her letters," said the Squire. "P'raps you could read the papers to her for a bit before she gets up, and so on."

"Does that take the whole morning?"

"No. She's down about twelve. Sometimes she goes for a ride then if she feels like it. Then either she goes out to lunch or someone lunches with us. And after that she's off in the car for a fifty-mile run—or a hundred if the mood takes her."

He drew a deep breath.

"She's never quiet—except when she's in bed. That's what I want you for. I want you to keep her quiet."

"Oh!" said Juliet.

This was shedding a new light upon the matter. She looked at him somewhat dubiously.

"Come! I know you can," he said. "You've got that sort of influence. I sensed it directly I saw you. You've got that priceless possession—a quiet spirit.

"All I want you to do is to put the brake on my wife, make her take an interest in her home, make her take life seriously. She's not at all strong, and she doesn't give herself a chance."

He spoke with bitter vehemence, beating restlessly against his heel with his whip.

"I have my ambitions, and I work for them. But the one thing I want more than anything else on earth is a son to succeed me. And if I can't have that—there's nothing else that counts."

Juliet still sat silently, looking out before her at the golden pink of the apple trees in the sunset light, with grave, quiet eyes.

He went on morosely, egotistically:

"I don't know what I've done that I shouldn't have what practically every labourer on my estate has got.

"I may not have been absolutely impeccable in my youth. I've never yet met a man who was—with the single exception of Dick Green, who hasn't much temptation to be anything else. But I've lived straight, on the whole. I've played the game—or tried to.

"And yet, after five years of marriage I'm still without an heir, and likely to remain so as far as I can see. She says I'm mad on that point."

He spoke resentfully.

"But, after all, it's what I married for. I don't see why I should be cheated out of the one thing I want most, do you?"

Juliet's eyes came up to his slowly, somewhat reluctantly.

"I'm afraid I haven't much sympathy with you," she said.

"You haven't?" He looked amazed.

"No." She paused a moment. "It was a pity you told me. You see, a woman doesn't care to be married . . . just for that."

"And what do you suppose she married me for?" he demanded indignantly. "Do you think she was in love with me—a man thirty years older than herself? Oh, I assure you there were never any illusions on that score! I had a good deal to offer her, and she jumped at it."

Juliet gave a slight shiver, and abruptly his manner changed.

"I'm sorry. Put my foot in it again, have I? You'll

have to forgive me, please. No, I shouldn't have told you.
But you've got such a kind look about you—as if you'd
understand."

He held out his hand to her abruptly.

"Look here! You're coming, aren't you?"

"I don't know," replied Juliet.

"Well, make up your mind quickly!" He held her
hand, looking at her. "What's the objection? Tell me!"

She freed her hand gently but with decision.

"I can't tell you at once. You must let me think."

She paused, then continued:

"For one thing, I want more freedom of action than I
should have as an inmate of your house. I want to come
and go as I like. I've never really done that before, and
I'm just beginning to enjoy it."

"That's a selfish reason," said the Squire, with a
sudden boyish grin at her.

She coloured slightly.

"No, it isn't . . . or not wholly."

"All right, it isn't. But that reason won't exist as far as
you are concerned. You will come and go exactly as you
like always. No-one will question you."

"You're very kind," said Juliet.

He bowed to her ceremoniously.

"That's the first really nice thing you have said to me.
I must make a note of it.

"Now, would you like my wife to call upon you? If
so, I'll send her round tomorrow at twelve."

He turned to go, pausing at the gate to throw her
another smiling farewell.

She had not thought that gloomy, black-browed
countenance could look so genial. There was something
curiously elusive, almost haunting, about his smile.

"Columbus!" said Juliet. "I'm not sure that he's a very
nice man, but there's something about him . . . something I
can't quite place . . . that makes me wonder if I've met
him somewhere before."

*   *   *

When the great high-powered car from Shale Court
stopped at the gate of the blacksmith's cottage the following morning, Mrs. Rickett was thrown into a state of wild
agitation.

She went nervously to enquire what was wanted, and met the Chauffeur at the gate.

"It's all right, Mrs. Rickett. Don't fluster yourself!" he said. "It's Miss Moore we're after. Go and tell her will you?"

Mrs. Rickett looked at the bold-eyed young man with disfavour.

"Well, you're not expecting her to come out to you, are you?" she retorted tartly.

He smiled.

"Yes, I rather think we are. Mrs. Fielding doesn't want to get out. Where is she?"

It was at this point that Juliet came upon the scene, walking up from the shore with her hair blowing in the breeze. She carried a towel and a bathing-dress on her arm.

She quickened her pace somewhat on seeing the car, and its occupant leant forward with an imperious motion of the hand.

"Miss Moore, I believe?" she said, in her slightly insolent tones.

Juliet came to the side of the car. The sun beat down upon her uncovered head. She smiled a welcome.

"How do you do? How kind of you to come and see me. Do come in!"

"Oh, I can't ... really!" protested Mrs. Fielding. "I shall die if I don't get a little air. I thought perhaps you would like to come for a spin with me."

"Thank you," replied Juliet. "I can be ready in five minutes."

In the schoolhouse garden she caught sight of a heavy, shambling figure, and waved a swift greeting as she flashed past.

"Oh, do you know that revolting youth?" asked Mrs. Fielding. "He's half-witted as well as deformed."

"His brother!" with a nod towards her Chauffeur's back. "He's a great trial to Jack, I believe.

"My husband," she went on, "has offered a hundred times to have him put into a home, but the other brother ... Green, the Schoolmaster ... is absolutely pig-headed on the subject, and won't hear of it."

"Poor Robin!" Juliet sighed. "I think he feels his deformity very much."

"Of course he does! He ought to be in a home among his own kind. It would be far better for everyone concerned. Frankly, the Green family exasperate me," declared Mrs. Fielding. "I can put up with Jack. He's such a smart, good-looking boy, and he can drive like the devil. But I've no use for the other two, and never shall have.

"As Dene Strange, the author, puts it, he is always hovering on the outside edge of every circle and ready to squeeze in at the very first opportunity."

"I should imagine my circle is hardly important enough to attract anyone in that way," remarked Juliet. "Strange is very caustic. I am not sure that I like him much."

"Oh, I enjoy him," said Mrs. Fielding. "He is so brilliant. You have never met him, I suppose?"

Juliet shook her head.

"Not under that name, anyway. But I haven't much sympathy with a man who hides behind a pseudonym; have you? It looks as if he hasn't the courage of his opinions."

"I shouldn't think anyone ever accused Dene Strange of lack of courage," retorted Mrs. Fielding. "I read all he writes. He is so intensely clever. I'd give a good deal to meet him."

"And be horribly disappointed," said Juliet.

"Why do you say that?"

"Because lions always are disappointing when they're hunted down. The ones that roar are quite insufferable, and the ones that don't are just banal."

Mrs. Fielding looked at her with interest for the first time.

"You speak as one who knows."

Juliet smiled.

"I have watched from the outside edge, as Dene Strange puts it. I expect you have heard of the Farringmores, haven't you? I am distantly related to them. I was brought up with Lady Joanna. So I know a little of what London people call 'life.'"

"I wonder you never married," said Mrs. Fielding.

"Do you?" Juliet spoke dreamily. "Lady Jo used to wonder that. But I've never yet met a man who was willing to wait, and I couldn't do a thing like that in a hurry."

"You could if you were in love," answered Mrs. Fielding.

"Yes, perhaps you're right. In that case, I have never been enough in love to take the leap." Juliet spoke with a half-smile. "But anyhow, Lady Jo couldn't talk, for she has just jilted Ivor Yardley, the Barrister."

"Good gracious!" exclaimed Mrs. Fielding. "Why, I saw the description of the wedding-dress in the paper the other day. It must have been a near thing."

"It was," said Juliet soberly. "They were to have been married today."

"And she broke it off! That must have taken some pluck!"

"But she didn't stay to face the music," Juliet pointed out. "That was what I hated in her. She ought to have stayed."

"Why didn't you go with her?" asked Mrs. Fielding.

Juliet made an odd gesture of the hands that was somehow passionate.

"Why should I? I have disapproved of her for a long time. I don't want to meet her ... or any of her set ... again!"

Mrs. Fielding was silent for a moment. She had not expected that intensity.

"Do you know, that doesn't sound like you, somehow," she said at length, speaking with just a hint of embarrassment.

"But how do you know what I am really like?" responded Juliet. "Ah! There is the sea again ... and the wonderful sky-line."

She spoke with a breathless little laugh. They had reached the summit of the great headland and it looked for the moment as if the car must leap over a sheer precipice into the clear green water far below.

Then they were standing still on a smooth stretch of grass not twenty feet from the edge.

The soft wind blew in their faces, and there was a glittering purity in the atmosphere that held Juliet spellbound. She breathed deeply, gazing far out over that sparkling sea.

After many seconds Juliet turned round.

"Thank you for bringing me here. It has done me good. I should like to stay here all day long."

Her eyes travelled along the line of cliff towards that distant spot that had been the scene of her night adventure, then slowly returned to dwell upon a long, deep seam in the side of the hill.

"That's the lead mine," observed Mrs. Fielding. "It belongs to your aristocratic relatives, the Farringmores. They are pretty badly hated by the miners, I believe.

"But your friend Mr. Green is extremely popular with them. He rather likes to be a King among cobblers, I imagine."

"How nice of him," said Juliet. "And where do the cobblers live?"

"You can't see it from here. It's just on the other side of the workings, a horribly squalid place. You can see the smoke hanging over there now."

She shuddered.

"The cottages are wretched places, and the people who live in them . . . words fail me! They are just like pigs in a sty."

"Poor dears!" said Juliet.

"Oh, they're horrors!" declared Mrs. Fielding. "They fling stones at the car if we go within half-a-mile of them. belongs to your aristocratic relatives, the Farringmores. Miss Moore will enjoy that."

"Thank you," said Juliet, with her friendly smile. "I am enjoying it very much."

They travelled forty miles before they ran back again into Little Shale, where the children were reassembling for afternoon school as they neared the Court gates.

"Put me down here!" Juliet said. "I can run down the hill. It isn't worthwhile coming those few yards and having to turn the car."

"I want you to lunch with me," said Mrs. Fielding.

"Oh, thank you very much. Not today. I really must get back. I've got to buy cakes for tea," said Juliet, with a laugh.

"I'm not going to press you, or you'll never come near me again," Mrs. Fielding went on. "Do you think you would hate living with me, Miss Moore? Or are you still giving the matter your consideration?"

There was a hint of wistfulness in the arrogant voice that somehow touched Juliet.

She was silent for a moment; then:

"If I might come to you for a week on trial," she said. "I think we should know by that time if it were likely to answer or not."

"When will you come?"

"Just when you like."

"Tomorrow?"

"Yes, tomorrow, if that suits you," answered Juliet.

"And if you don't hate me at the end of a week you'll come for good?"

Juliet laughed.

"No, I won't say that. I'll leave you a way of escape too. We will see how it answers."

Mrs. Fielding held out her hand.

"Good-bye! Next time you take your tea on the shore, I want to be the guest of honour."

"You shall be," answered Juliet.

Chapter
Three

"Everyone to his taste," remarked Mr. Green. "But I'd rather be anything under the sun than Mrs. Fielding's paid Companion."

He glanced at Juliet with a smile as he spoke, but there was a certain earnestness in his speech that told her he meant what he said.

"Don't let them bully you!"

She smiled.

"No, they won't do that. I think it is rather kind of them to take me without any references, don't you?"

"No," replied Mr. Green.

She turned and surveyed him with a gleam of amusement.

"You sound cross! Are you cross about anything?"

His eyes flashed down to hers with a suddenness that was almost startling. He did not speak for a moment; then again he smiled abruptly, with his eyes still holding hers.

"I believe I am."

"I wonder why," said Juliet.

His dark, alert face looked strangely swarthy against the rock behind him. His expression was one of open discontent.

"I hate to think of you turning into that woman's slave," he said abruptly. "To be quite honest, that was what brought me along today, intruding upon your picnic with Robin. I want to warn you. I've got to warn you."

"You have warned me."

"But you won't profit by it." Mr. Green's voice was moody.

"I think I shall. In any case, I am only going for a week on trial. That couldn't hurt anyone."

He did not look at her.

"You're going out of the goodness of your heart. And—though you won't like it—you'll stay for the same reason."

"Oh, don't you think you are rather absurd?" asked Juliet. "I am not at all that sort of person, I assure you."

"I think you are."

She laughed again.

"Well, I am told you are quite a frequent visitor there. Why do you go . . . if you don't like it?"

"That is different. I can hold my own—anyway, with Mr. Fielding."

She lifted her brows.

"And you think I can't?"

"You'll hate it," he retorted with conviction.

"I don't think I shall," she answered quietly. "If I do, I shall come away."

"It'll be too late then."

"Too late!" Juliet's soft eyes opened wide. "What can you mean?"

He made a gesture which, though half-restrained, was yet vehement.

"It's a hostile atmosphere—a hateful atmosphere. She will poison you with her sneers and snobbery!"

A light began to break upon Juliet. She sat up very suddenly.

"Oh, I quite catch your meaning, Mr. Green. But . . . really, I am not in the habit of listening to sneers against my friends. Now will you be satisfied?"

He laughed also, though still with a touch of restraint.

"Yes, I feel better for that. You are so royal in your ways. I might have known I was safe there."

" 'Loyal' is a better word, I think," replied Juliet quietly. "Why should a paid Companion aspire to be any higher on the social scale than a village Schoolmaster? Do you think occupation really makes any difference?"

"Theoretically—no."

"Neither theoretically nor practically," said Juliet. "I

detest snobbery, so do you. If you came to the Court to sweep the kitchen chimney I should be just as pleased to see you. What a man does is nothing. How could it make any difference?"

"It couldn't—to you," responded Mr. Green.

"Or to you?" said Juliet.

He laughed a little, his black brows working comically.

"Madam, if I met you hawking stale fish for cat's meat in the public street I couldn't venerate you more or adore you less. Whatever you do—is right."

"Good heavens!" said Juliet, and flushed in spite of herself. "What a magnificent compliment! Mr. Green, what can have happened to you?"

"I daren't tell you," he replied.

A sudden silence fell upon the words.

"Well, don't spoil it, will you?" she asked.

His hand suddenly gripped a handful of shingle and ground it forcibly. He did not speak for a second or two.

"No, I won't spoil it," he said in a low voice.

A moment later he flung the stones abruptly from him and got up.

"You're not going?" asked Juliet.

"Yes, I've got work to do. Shall I take Robin with me?"

There was a dogged note in his voice. His eyes avoided hers.

Juliet rose slowly.

"Never mind Robin! Walk a little way with me!"

"I think I'd better go," he replied restlessly.

"Please!" said Juliet gently.

He turned beside her without a word. They went down the shingle to the edge of the sand and began to walk along the shore.

For many seconds they walked in silence. Juliet's eyes were fixed upon the mighty outline of High Shale Point, which stood out like a fortress, dark and impregnable, against the calm of the evening sky.

She spoke at length, slowly, with evident effort.

"I want to tell you ... something ... about myself."

"Something I really don't know?" he asked, his dark face flashing to a smile.

There was no answering smile on Juliet's face.

"Yes, something you don't know. It's just this. I have much more in common with Mrs. Fielding than you have any idea of. I have lived for pleasure practically all my life. I have scrambled for happiness with the rest of the world, and I haven't found it."

She paused, then continued:

"It's only just lately that I've realised why. I read a book called *The Valley of Dry Bones*. It is by Dene Strange. I hate his work . . . the bitter cynicism of it, the merciless exposure of humanity at its lowest and meanest.

"I don't know what his ideals are . . . if he has any. I burnt the book. I hated it so. But I felt . . . afterwards . . . as if I had been burnt, seared by hot irons . . . ashamed . . . most cruelly ashamed."

Juliet's voice sank almost to a whisper.

"Because life really is like that, one vast structure of selfishness . . . and in many ways I have helped to make it so."

She stopped. He was looking at her attentively. He spoke at once with decision.

"I know the book. I've read it. It's an exaggeration—probably intentional. It wasn't written—obviously—for the super-sensitive."

"Wasn't it?" Juliet's lips were quivering. "Well, it's been a positive nightmare to me. I haven't got over it yet."

"That's curious," he replied. "I shouldn't have thought it could have touched you anywhere."

"That is because you have a total wrong impression of me," she said. "That is what I am trying to put right. I am the sort of person that horrible book applies to, and I've fallen out with myself very badly in consequence, Mr. Green. I haven't told anyone but you, but . . . somehow . . . I feel as if you ought to know."

"Thank you," he answered. "But why?"

She met his eyes very steadily.

"Because I'm trying to play the game now, and . . . I don't want you to have any illusions."

"You don't want me to make a fool of myself. Is that it?"

She coloured very vividly, but she did not avoid his look.

"I don't think there is much danger of that, is there?"

He stood still and faced her. His eyes burnt with an amazing brightness.

"I don't know," he said, speaking emphatically and very rapidly. "But I'll tell you this. I'd give all I've got to prevent you from going to Shale Court as a Companion."

She looked at him in perplexity.

"But it wouldn't be fair to draw back now," she objected. "Besides . . ."

"Besides," he broke in almost fiercely, "you've got your living to make, like the rest of us."

He ground his heel deep into the yielding sand.

"My God! What wouldn't I give for the privilege of working for you?"

The words were uttered and beyond recall. He looked her straight in the face as he spoke them, but an instant later he turned and stared out over the wide, calm sea.

Juliet stood silently, almost as if she were waiting for him to recover his balance. Her eyes also were gazing straight before her to that far, mysterious sky-line. They were very grave and rather sad.

He broke the silence after many seconds.

"You will never speak to me again after this."

"I hope I shall," she said gently.

He wheeled and faced her.

"You're not angry, then?"

She shook her head.

His eyes flashed over her with amazing swiftness.

"I almost wish you were."

"But why?" she asked.

"Because I should know then that it mattered a little. Now I know it doesn't. I am just one of the many. Isn't that it? There are so many of us that one more or one less doesn't count either way."

He laughed ruefully.

"Well, I won't repeat the offence. Even your patience must have its limits. Shall we go back?"

It was then that Juliet turned, moved by an impulse so urgent that she could not pause to analyse it. She held out her hand to him, quickly, shyly, and as he gripped and held it she spoke, her voice tremulous, breathless, barely coherent.

"I am not offended. I am . . . very . . . very . . . deeply . . . honoured. Only, you . . . don't understand."

He kept her hand closely in his own. His grasp vibrated with electric force, but he had himself in check.

"You are more generous than I deserve," he said, his voice sinking to a whisper. "Perhaps, someday, understanding will come. May I hope for that?"

She did not answer him, but for one intimate second her eyes looked straight into his. Then with a sobbing little breath she slipped her hand free.

*   *   *

Robin was in disgrace. He crouched in a sulky heap in a far corner of the schoolroom and glowered across the empty desks and benches at his elder brother, who sat at his writing-table with a litter of untidy exercise-books in front of him.

Richard Green lifted his eyes from his work and sent a keen, flashing glance down the long, bare room.

"Robin!" he said. "Get up and come here!"

Robin grabbed at the end of the row of desks nearest to him and dragged himself up slowly. He moved forward, dragging his feet along the bare boards. At the other end of the row of desks he halted.

Across the writing-table Richard Green faced him. He said, very distinctly:

"Why did you throw that stone at Mrs. Fielding's car?"

Robin was trembling from head to foot. He drew a quivering breath between his teeth, and stood silently.

"Tell me why," his brother persisted.

Robin locked his hands together.

"It—it—I didn't see—Mrs. Fielding," he blurted out. "I didn't mean to break the window, Dicky."

"What did you mean to do, then?"

Robin stood silently again.

"Are you going to answer me?" Richard Green asked, after a pause.

For several moments a tense silence reigned.

Then he said quietly:

"Oh, yes you will. Sit down there!"

He indicated the end of the bench nearest to him.

"I'll deal with you presently."

He went back to his correcting, with a frown between his brows, and a deep silence fell.

Minutes passed. The room grew darker, the atmosphere more leaden. Pencil in hand, Richard Green went over book after book and put them aside. Suddenly he looked across at the silent figure.

Slow tears were falling upon the clasped hands. There was no sound of any sort. Richard Green sat and watched, a kind of stern pity replacing the unyielding mastery of his look. He moved at length, and was on the verge of speaking, when something checked him.

Footsteps fell beyond the open door, and in a moment a man's figure appeared, entering through the gloom.

"Hullo, Dick!" a voice said. "There's going to be a devil of a storm. Where's that Robin?"

Richard Green rose with a sharp movement.

"Jack! I want a word with you. Come outside!"

He passed Robin and went to the newcomer, gripping him quickly by the shoulder and turning him back the way he had come.

Jack submitted to the imperative touch. He was taller and broader than his elder brother, but he lacked that subtle something, the distinction of bearing, which in Richard Green was very apparent.

"Well, Dick! What do you want?" he said. "I'm pretty mad, I can tell you. I hope you're going to thrash him well. Because if you don't, I shall."

Briefly and decidedly Dick answered:

"No, you won't. You'll not touch him. I shall do whatever is necessary."

"Shall you?" retorted Jack. "Then why don't you shut him up in a home? It's the only place he's fit for."

"Shut up, please!" Dick's tone was an odd mixture of tolerance and exasperation. "I'll manage this affair my own way. But I've got to know the truth of it first. What made him throw that stone?"

"Oh yes, I can tell you that. He's taken to haunting the place—the Court, mind you—to lie in wait for the fair Juliet. She's been too kind to him, and now he dogs her footsteps whenever he gets a chance.

"I caught him this afternoon, right up by the house,

and I ordered him off. And I told him what he was and where to go to, and I presume he thought he'd send me there first. There you have it all—cause and effect."

"Thank you," replied Dick.

He paused a moment, looking speculatively at Jack's complacent face.

"It was a pity you were so damned offensive, but I suppose it's the way you're made. You were the sole cause of the whole thing, and if there's any decency in you, you'll go and tell the Squire so."

"Confound you!" blustered Jack. "You expect me to go to the Squire and tell him it was my fault, do you?"

"No. I don't expect it in the least!" Dick almost laughed. "In fact, nothing would surprise me more. Thank you for telling me the truth. Do you mind clearing out now? I don't want you in here."

His curt, cold tone fell like ice on flame. Jack swore a muffled oath and turned away. There was no-one in the world who possessed the power to humble him as did Dick, who with a few scorching words could make him writhe in impotent fury.

Dick turned back into the schoolroom with deep lines between his brows, but implacable determination in his every movement, a determination that was not directed against the poor cowering form that crouched waiting for him.

Robin looked up at his coming, drawing himself together with a nervous contraction of the muscles like the mute shrinking of an abject dog.

Dick bent suddenly and laid a quieting hand upon him.

"Robin, do you know you've got me into bad trouble?"

Robin knelt by his side.

"Will it cost much?" he asked.

"The window, you mean? Well, not so much as if you had broken Jack's head—as you intended.

"You've got to stop it, Robin," he went on, firmly. "If you don't, there'll be trouble—worse trouble than you've had yet."

A sudden hard shudder caught him. He shook it off impatiently, and turned to the quivering figure still kneeling in the circle of his arm.

He gripped it suddenly close.

"There's a sort of hell these fiendish tempers of yours might end in. You've got to save yourself. I can't save you."

Robin clung to him tensely, desperately.

"You don't want me to leave you, do you, Dicky?" he whispered.

"Good God! Of course not!"

In the silence that followed, Robin turned with a curious groping movement, took the hand that pressed his shoulder, and pulled it over his eyes.

* * *

An ominous darkness brooded over all things as Richard Green walked up the long avenue of Shale Court half-an-hour later.

He was halfway up the drive when the first flash of lightning glimmered eerily across the heavy gloom.

It was followed so swiftly by a burst of thunder that he realised that he had no time to spare if he hoped to escape the threatening deluge.

He broke into a run, covering the ground with the ease of a practised athlete. But he was not destined to run to a finish.

As he rounded a bend that gave him a view of the house in the distance, he suddenly heard a voice call to him from the deep shadow of the trees, and checking sharply he discerned a dim figure coming towards him.

He diverted his course without a moment's thought, and went to meet it.

"Ah, how kind of you!" said Juliet. "And there's going to be such a downpour in a minute."

"What is the matter?" he asked.

She was smiling a difficult smile.

"Nothing very much. I have given my foot a stupid twist, that's all."

"Take my arm!"

She took it, her white face still bravely smiling. "Thank you, Mr. Green. It really is a shame. We shall both be drenched now."

He glanced at the threatening sky.

"It may hold off for a bit yet. What were you doing?"

"I was coming to see you."

"To see me!" He looked swiftly at her. "What about?"

"About Robin," she answered simply. "I wasn't in the car when it happened, but I heard all about it when Mrs. Fielding came in. Mr. Green, I hope you haven't been very hard on him."

Richard Green was silent for a moment, then said:

"And you started straight off to come to the rescue?"

"Oh, I felt so sure that he acted on impulse. You can't judge him by ordinary standards. It isn't fair," pleaded Juliet. "There was probably some extenuating circumstance, something we don't know about. I hope you haven't been very severe."

He began to smile.

"You make me out an awful ogre. No, I haven't punished him at all. As you say, we must be fair, and I found he wasn't the person most to blame. Can you guess who was?"

"No."

"I thought not. Well, I have traced it to its souce, and it lies at your door."

"At mine!" ejaculated Juliet.

"At yours, yes. You've been too kind to him. It's just your way, isn't it? You spoil everybody."

Again for an instant his look flashed over her.

"With the result that Robin lies in wait on forbidden ground for a glimpse of his divinity. Being caught and roundly abused for it by his brother Jack, he naturally took offence, and trouble ensued. That is the whole story."

"Oh, dear!" Juliet sighed. "But surely that was very unnecessary of your brother Jack! He might have made allowances."

"My brother Jack never makes allowances for anyone but himself," he replied drily.

A sudden vivid flash rent the gloom above them, and Juliet caught her breath. There followed a burst of thunder that seemed to shake the very foundations of the earth. Great drops of rain began to splash round them.

"Quick!" gasped Juliet. "We can't ... possibly ...

reach the house now. There is an arbour ... by the garden gate. Let's go there!"

Again a jagged line of light gleamed before them. Again the thunder crashed. They found the little gate and the arbour beyond.

"Thank goodness!" Juliet gasped.

She stumbled at the step of the summer-house, and he thrust an arm forward to catch her. He almost lifted her into shelter. The darkness within was complete. She leant upon him, trembling.

"You're not hurt?"

"No, not hurt, only ... shaken ... and ... and ... stupid," she answered, on the verge of tears.

His arm still held her. It closed about her, very surely, very steadily. He did not utter a word.

The rain swept down in a torrent, as if the skies had opened. The noise of the downpour seemed vaster, more overwhelming, even than the thunder.

Juliet was palpitating from head to foot. She leant upon the supporting arm, her eyes closed against the leaping lightning, her two hands pressed hard upon her breast.

And the man's arm drew her nearer, nearer, till she felt the strong beating of his heart.

Slowly the turmoil abated. The downpour lessened. The storm passed. And Juliet stirred.

"I'm not generally so foolish as this," she murmured. "But it was so very violent."

"I know," he answered.

His hold slackened. He let her go. And then suddenly he stayed her. He took her hand and, bending, pressed it closely, burningly, to his lips.

She stood motionless, suffering him. But in a moment, as he still held her, very gently she spoke.

"Mr. Green, please ... don't be so terribly in earnest! It's too soon. I warned you before. You haven't known me ... long enough."

He stood up and faced her, her hand still in his. A light was growing behind the storm-clouds, revealing his dark, clean-cut features, and the look, half-humorous, half-tense, that rested upon them.

"Yes, I know you warned me," he said rather jerkily.

"I quite realise that it's my funeral—not yours. I shan't ask you to be chief mourner either. I've always considered that when a man makes a fool of himself over a woman, it's up to him to bear the consequences without asking her to share them."

"But we're not talking of funerals."

"Aren't we?" His hand tightened for a moment upon hers. "I thought we were. What is it, then?"

She smiled at him with a whimsical sadness in the weird storm-light.

"I think there are a good many names for it. I call it midsummer madness, myself."

He made a quick gesture of protest.

"Do you? Oh, I know a better name than that. But you don't want to hear it. I believe you are afraid of me. It sounds preposterous, but I believe you are."

Her hand stirred within his, but not as though seeking to escape.

"No, I don't think so," she answered, and in her voice was a sound as if laughter and tears were striving together for the mastery.

"But I'm trying," she went on, "so dreadfully hard . . . to be discreet. I don't want you to let yourself go too far. It's so difficult . . . you don't know how difficult it is to get back afterwards."

"Good heavens! Don't you realise that I passed the turning-back stage long ago?"

"Oh, I hope not," she said quickly. "I hope not!"

"Then I am afraid you are doomed to disappointment. But I am sure you are far too sensible—discreet, I mean—to let that worry you."

She glanced at him, for his tone was baffling.

"And you don't think me quite heartless?"

He bent towards her.

"No," he answered, and though he smiled as in duty bound, she caught a deep throb in his voice that pierced straight through her. "I love you all the better for it."

Then, before she could find words to protest, he went on:

"I say, I believe it's left off raining. Hadn't we better go while we can?"

She turned to look. A pale light was shining from the western sky. The storm was over. The raindrops glittered

in the growing radiance. The whole earth seemed transformed.

"Yes, let us go!" she said, and stepped down into a
world of crystal-clearness.

He followed her, his face uplifted to the scattering
drops, moving with a free and faun-like spring that
seemed to mark him as a being closely allied to Nature,
curiously vital yet also curiously self-restrained.

She did not look at him again, but as they passed
together through the wonderland which with every moment was growing to a more amazing brightness, she told
herself that there was little of midsummer madness about
this man's emotions.

Jest as he might, she knew by instinct that he was
vitally in earnest, and she had a strange conviction that it
was for the first time in his life. The certainty disquieted
her. Had she fled from one danger to another, she who
asked only for peace?

But she reassured herself with the thought that he
had held her against his heart, and he had not sought to
take her. That forbearance of his gave him a greatness in
her eyes which no other man had ever attained.

And gradually a sense of security to which she was
little accustomed came about her heart and comforted her.
She had warned him. Surely he understood?

*   *   *

Almost in silence they passed up through the dripping garden to the house, side-by-side, Columbus trotting
demurely behind. Juliet was still limping, but she would
not accept support.

"I suppose you are going to beard the lion in his
den," she said as they drew near.

"I suppose I am," he answered. "If you hear sounds
of a serious fracas, perhaps you will come to the rescue."

"Not to yours," she responded lightly. "You are more
than capable of holding your own . . . anywhere."

He flashed her his sudden look.

"Do you really think so? I assure you I am considered
very small fry indeed in this household."

"That's very good for you."

They mounted to the terrace that bounded the south

front of the house, and entered by a glass door that led into a Conservatory. Here for a moment Juliet paused. Her grey eyes under their level brows met his with a friendly smile.

"I think I must leave you now, Mr. Green, and go and find Mrs. Fielding. I expect the Squire is in his study."

She threw him a nod, cool and kindly, over her shoulder, and departed.

He watched her disappear into the room beyond, Columbus in close attendance. Then for a few seconds his hands went up to his face, and he stood motionless, pressing his temples hard, feeling the blood surging with feverish heat through his veins.

How marvellous she was, and how gracious! How had he dared? Midsummer madness, indeed! And yet she had suffered him!

A great shaft of red sunlight burst suddenly through the heaped storm-clouds in the west. He turned and faced it, dazzled but strangely exultant. He felt as if his whole being had been plunged into the glowing flame.

Then he turned, as if the glory had become too much for him, and went into the house.

He had been well acquainted with the place from boyhood, though since the Squire's marriage he had ceased to enter it unannounced.

Before his appointment to the village school he had acted for a time as the Squire's secretary, but it had never been more than a temporary arrangement, and it had come to a speedy end when Mrs. Fielding became Mistress of the Court.

Between her and her husband's protégé, as she scornfully called him, there had always existed a very decided antipathy.

The room he entered was empty. He passed through it without a pause and found himself in the great Entrance Hall. He crossed this to a door on the other side, and, knocking briefly, opened it without waiting for a reply.

Mr. Fielding was seated in a leather arm-chair, reading a newspaper. He looked at his visitor over it with anything but a favourable eye.

"What have you come for?" he asked.

Richard Green halted in front of him.

"I've come to make a very humble apology, for my boy Robin's misdemeanour."

Mr. Fielding sat motionless, still looking up at Richard Green from under heavily scowling brows.

"Do you think I'm going to be satisfied with just an apology?"

"May I sit down, please?" queried Richard Green, pulling forward a chair.

"Oh, yes, sit down! Sit down and argue!" said the Squire irritably. "You're always ready with some plausible excuse for that half-witted young scoundrel."

He scowled.

"I'll tell you, Dick if you don't get rid of him after this, there'll be a split between us. I'm not going to countenance your infernal obstinacy any longer. The boy is unsafe, and he must go."

Dick's eyes, very bright, wholly undismayed, continued to meet his with unvarying steadiness.

"I'm very sorry, Sir. The answer is the same as usual. I can't."

"Won't, you mean!" There was a sound in the Squire's voice like the muffled roar of an angry animal.

Dick's black brows travelled swiftly upwards and came down again.

"The boy is as harmless as any of us if he isn't baited. There was a reason for what he did today. I'm not going into details. But you may take it from me—he was provoked."

"Oh! Was he!" ejaculated the Squire. "And who provoked him? Jack?"

Dick hesitated momentarily.

"Yes, Jack," he said briefly. "He has some reason, but he's such a tactless ass. He blames Robin, of course. Everyone always does."

"Except you," replied the Squire drily. "Oh, and Miss Moore! She makes excuses for him at every turn."

He suddenly laid a hand on the younger man's arm, gripping it mercilessly.

"Look here, Richard." His voice changed abruptly. "I'm not ordering, I'm asking. That boy is a millstone round your neck. Give him up like a dear chap! Then you'll be free—free to make your own way in the world— free to marry and be happy."

Dick made a slight movement under the hand that held him, but he did not attempt to speak.

Again, more gently, the Squire shook the shoulder under his hand.

"I'm out to make you happy, Dick. Can't you see it? For your mother's sake as well as your own.

"And there's a chance coming your way now—or I'm much mistaken—she's just the woman for you. And you can't ask her as long as you keep that half-witted creature dangling after you. It wouldn't be right, man, even if she'd have you."

The Squire's tone was grim.

"It would be a hopeless handicap to any marriage— an insurmountable obstacle to happiness, hers as well as yours. For heaven's sake, let him go!"

He ceased to speak, and there fell a silence so tense, so electric, that it seemed as if it must mask something terrible.

Dick's face was still immovable, but he had the look of a man who endures unutterable things. He had flinched once, and only once, during the Squire's speech, and that was at the first mention of Juliet.

But for the rest he had stood quite rigidly, as he stood now, his lips tightly compressed, his eyes looking straight before him.

He came out of his silence at last with a movement so sudden that it was as if he flung aside some weight that threatened to overwhelm him.

The arrested vitality flashed back into his face. He threw back his head with a smile, and looked the Squire in the face.

"You haven't left me with a leg to stand on, Sir," he said. "But all the same—I stand. There's nothing more to be said, except—may I pay for the window?"

The Squire's hand dropped from his shoulder.

"You're very cussed," he said finally. "I wish I'd had the upbringing of you."

Dick laughed.

"Well, you've meddled in my affairs as long as I can

remember, Sir. I don't know anyone who has had as much to do with me as you have."

"And precious little satisfaction I've got out of it," grumbled the Squire. "You've always been a kicker."

He broke off as a knock came at the door, and turned away with an impatient fling.

"Who is it? Come in!"

The door opened. Juliet stood on the threshold. The evening light fell full upon her. She was dressed in cloudy grey that fell about her in soft folds. Her face was flushed but quite serene.

"Mrs. Fielding wants to know if you have forgotten dinner."

The Squire's face changed magically. He smiled upon Juliet.

"Come in, Miss Moore! You've met this pestilent pedagogue before, I think."

"Just once or twice," Juliet answered, coming forward.

"How is the ankle?" Richard Green asked.

She smiled at him without embarrassment.

"Oh, better, thank you. It was only a wrench."

"Hurt yourself?" questioned the Squire.

"No, no. It's really nothing. I slipped in the Park and nearly sprained my ankle . . . just not quite," replied Juliet. "And Mr. Green very kindly helped me into shelter."

"Did he?" said the Squire, and looked at Richard Green searchingly. "Well, Mr. Green, you'd better stay and dine, as you are here."

"You're very kind," Dick said. "I don't know whether I ought. I'm not dressed."

"Of course you ought!" replied the Squire testily. "Come on and wash! Your clothes won't matter—we're alone. That is, if Miss Moore doesn't object."

"I have no objection whatever," responded Juliet.

She was looking from one to the other with a slightly puzzled expression.

"What is it?" asked the Squire, pausing.

His look was kindly. Juliet laughed.

"I don't know. I feel as I felt that day you caught me trespassing. Am I trespassing, I wonder?"

"No," both men replied in one breath.

She swept them a deep Court curtsey.

"Thank you, gentlemen! With your leave I will now withdraw."

The Squire was at the door. He bowed her out with ceremony, watched her cross the Hall, then sharply turned his head.

Richard Green was watching her also, but, keen as the twist of a rapier in the hand of a practised fencer, his eyes flashed to meet the Squire's.

The Squire smiled grimly. He motioned him forward, gripped him by the arm, and drew him out of the room. They mounted the shallow oak stairs side-by-side.

At the top, in a tense whisper, the Squire spoke.

"Don't you be a fool, Richard! Don't you be a damn fool!"

Dick's laugh had in it a note that was not of mirth.

"All right, Sir. I'll do my best."

It was a drawn battle, and they both knew it. By tacit consent neither referred to the matter again.

Chapter
Four

"How like my husband!" said Mrs. Fielding impatiently, fidgeting up and down the long Drawing-Room with a fretful frown on her pretty face.

"Why didn't you put a stop to it, Miss Moore? You might so easily have said that the storm had upset me and I wasn't equal to a visitor at the dinner-table tonight."

She paused to look at herself in the gilded mirror above the mantelpiece.

"I declare I look positively haggard. I've a good mind to go to bed."

"Good-evening," said Richard Green's voice, from the doorway. "How do you do, Mrs. Fielding? As I can't dress, I've been sent down to try and make my peace with you for showing my face here at all."

He came forward with the words. His bearing was absolutely easy, though neither he nor his hostess seemed to think of shaking hands.

She looked at him with a disdainful curve of the lips that could scarcely have been described as a smile of welcome.

She turned as if Richard Green's proximity were an offence to her, and walked away to the window at the farther end of the room.

In the slightly strained pause that followed, Juliet bent to fondle Columbus, who was sitting pressed against her, and her book slid from her lap to the ground. Richard Green stooped swiftly and picked it up.

"What is it? May I look?"

She held out her hand for it.

"It is *Marionettes* ... Dene Strange's latest. Mrs. Fielding lent it to me."

He kept the book in his hand.

"I thought you said you wouldn't read any more of that man's stuff."

She knitted her brows a little.

"Did I say so? I don't remember."

He looked down at her keenly.

"You said you hated the man and his work."

She began to smile.

"Well, I do ... in certain moods. But I've got to read him, all the same. Everyone does."

"Surely you don't follow the crowd?"

She laughed, her sweet, low laugh.

"Surely I do! I'm one of them."

He made a sharp gesture.

"That's just what you are not. I say, Miss Moore, don't read this book! It won't do you any good, and it'll make you very angry. You'll call it cynical, insincere, cold-blooded. It will hurt your feelings horribly."

"I don't think so," said Juliet. "You forget ... I am no longer ... a marionette. I have come to life."

Again she held out her hand for the book. He gave it to her reluctantly.

"Don't read it!"

She shook her head, still smiling.

"No, Mr. Green, I'm not going to let you censor my reading. I will tell you what I think of it next time we meet."

Mrs. Fielding looked round from the windows and spoke fretfully.

"The storm seems to have made it more oppressive than ever," she complained. "I believe it is coming up again."

"I hope not," replied Richard Green.

Juliet got up quietly and moved to join her—a tall woman of gracious outlines with the poise of a Princess.

"You know all about everything," she said to him in passing. "Come and read the weather for us!"

He followed her. They stood together at the open French window, looking out at the stormy sunset.

"It isn't coming back," said Richard Green after a pause. "We shall have a fine day for the Graydown races tomorrow."

"Are you keen on racing?" asked Juliet.

He laughed.

"I've no time for frivolities of that sort."

"You could make time if you wanted to," observed Mrs. Fielding. "You are free on Saturday."

"Am I?"

She challenged him in sudden exasperation:

"Well, what do you do on your off days?"

He considered for a moment.

"I'll tell you what I'm doing tomorrow, if you like. In the morning I hold a swimming-class for all who care to attend. In the afternoon I've got a cricket-match. And in the evening I'm running an open-air concert at High Shale with Ashcott."

"For those wretched miners!" exclaimed Mrs. Fielding. "Those High Shale people are so hopelessly disreputable, such a drunken, lawless lot."

"But not beyond redemption," said Richard Green quickly, "if anyone takes the trouble."

"Tell me about the cricket-match," Juliet said, intervening. "Who is playing?"

He gave her a glance of quizzical understanding.

"Oh, that's a village affair too. I have the honour to be Captain of the Little Shale team."

"You seem to be everything," she responded.

"Jack of all trades!" sneered Mrs. Fielding.

Richard Green laughed.

"I was just going to say that."

"How original of you!" said Juliet. "Well, I hope you'll win."

"He is the sort of person who always comes out on top whether he wins or loses," said the Squire, striding up the long room at that moment. "Where are you playing, Dick?"

His good humour was evidently fully restored. He slapped a hand on Dick's shoulder with the words. Mrs. Fielding's lips turned downwards at the action.

"We are playing the Fairharbour crowd, Sir, on Lord Saltash's ground."

"Yes, yes, I know it. A fine place. Pity it doesn't belong to somebody decent," replied the Squire.

Mrs. Fielding laughed unpleasantly.

"Dear me! More wicked Lords?"

Her husband looked at her with his quick frown.

"I thought everyone knew Saltash was a scoundrel. It's common talk that he's in Paris at this moment entertaining that worthless jade, Lady Joanna Farringmore."

Juliet gave a violent start at the words. For a moment her face flamed red, then went dead white—so white that she looked almost as if she would faint.

Then, in a very low voice, she said:

"It may be common talk, but I am quite sure it isn't true."

"Good heavens!" exclaimed the Squire. "My dear Miss Moore, pray forgive me! I forgot you knew her."

She smiled at him, still with that ashen face.

"Yes, I know her. At least . . . I used to. And she may have been heartless . . . I think she was . . . but she wasn't . . . that."

"Not when you knew her, perhaps," said Mrs. Fielding scornfully.

She had no sympathy with people who regarded it as a duty to stand up for their unworthy friends.

"But since you quarrelled with her yourself on account of her disgraceful behaviour, you are scarcely in a position to defend her."

"No . . . I know," answered Juliet, and she spoke nervously, painfully. "But . . . I must defend her on a point of honour."

She did not look at Richard Green. Yet instantly and very decidedly he entered the breach.

"Quite so. We are all entitled to fair play—though we don't always get it when our backs are turned. I take off my hat to you, Miss Moore, for your loyalty to your friends."

She gave him a quick glance without speaking.

From the door the Butler announced dinner, and they all turned.

"Miss Moore, I apologise," said the Squire, and offered her his arm.

She took it, her hand not very steady.

"Please forget it," she said.

He smiled at her kindly as he led her from the room, and began to speak of other things.

Richard Green sauntered behind with his hostess His eyes were extremely bright, and he made no attempt to make conversation as he went.

* * *

It was an unpleasant shock to Juliet, on the following morning when she went to Mrs. Fielding's room after breakfast, to find her lying in bed, pale and tear-stained, refusing morosely to partake of any nourishment whatever.

"Why, what is the matter?" said Juliet.

"I've had a wretched night," Mrs. Fielding answered, and turned her face into the pillow with a sob.

Juliet bent over her, discarding all ceremony.

"My dear girl, do stop. What on earth is the matter? You won't get over it all day if you go on like this."

"I don't care if I die!" cried Mrs. Fielding, with a fresh burst of weeping. "I'm miserable . . . miserable! And nobody cares!"

She flung herself down upon the pillow in such a paroxysm of hysterical sobbing that Juliet actually was alarmed. She stood beside her, impotent, unable to make herself heard, and wondered what to do.

To her astonishment, the door suddenly opened and the Squire himself appeared on the threshold.

She turned sharply, her first impulse to keep him out, for he wore an ugly look.

"Vera," he said, "stop it at once! Do you hear me? Stop it."

He did not raise his voice, but his words had a pitiless distinction that seemed somehow more forcible than any violence. Vera Fielding shrank closer to Juliet's breast.

"Don't leave me! Don't leave me," she moaned, still shaken from head to foot with great sobs she could not control.

"Hush!" Juliet said. "Don't you know there isn't a man living who can stand this? Be quiet, my dear, for heaven's sake! You're making the most hideous mistake of your life."

She spoke with most unwonted force, and again the Squire's steady eyes shot upwards, regarding her piercingly.

"You're quite right," he said briefly. "I won't stand it. I've stood too much already. Now, Vera, you behave yourself, and stop that crying—at once!"

There was that in his tone that quelled all rebellion. Vera shrank closer to Juliet, but she began to make some feeble efforts to subdue her wild distress.

The Squire sat on the edge of the bed, her hand firmly in his, and waited. His expression was one of absolute and implacable determination. He looked so forbidding and so formidable that Juliet wondered a little at her own temerity in remaining.

She decided then and there that a serious disagreement with the Squire would be too great a tax upon any woman's strength, and she did not wonder that Vera's had broken down under it.

The Squire frowned heavily, his eyes grimly, piercingly, upon Juliet.

She met his look with steady resolution.

"Won't you leave her to rest for a little while? I think she needs it."

"Very well," he replied, and though he did not look like he would yield, she realised to her surprise that he had done so.

He turned to the door.

"I should like a word with you in the Library," he said, as he reached it. "Please come to me there immediately!"

Juliet realised as she descended the stairs that her heart was beating uncomfortably hard, but she did not pause on that account. She wanted to face the Squire while her spirit was high.

She held her head up as she entered the Library, but when he turned sharply from the window to meet her she was conscious of a moment of most undignified dread.

Whether her face betrayed her or not she never knew, but she was aware in an instant of a change in his attitude.

He came straight up to her, and suddenly her hand was in his and he was looking into her eyes with the gleam of a smile in his own.

"Come along!" he said. "Let's have it! I'm the biggest brute you ever came across, and you never want to set eyes on me again. Isn't that it?"

It was winningly spoken, restoring her self-confidence in a second. She shook her head in answer.

"No, I'm not in a position to judge, and I don't think I want to be. I have no real liking for meddling in other people's affairs."

"Very wise!" he commented.

He paused, looking at her under his black brows as if debating with himself as to how far he would take her into his confidence.

"I've been cheated of the best from the very outset," he said, "cheated and thwarted at every turn."

He fell to pacing up and down the room, staring moodily at the floor, his hands behind him.

"Life is such an infernal gamble at the best," he went on, "but I never had a chance. It's been one damn thing after another. I've tripped at every hurdle. I suppose you never came a cropper in your life—don't know what it means."

"I think I do know what it means," Juliet answered slowly. "I've looked on, you know. I've seen . . . a good many things."

"Just as you're looking on now, eh?" said the Squire, grimly smiling. "Well, you profit by my experience—if you can! And if love ever comes your way, hang on to it, even if you drop everything else to do it! It's the gift of the gods, my dear, and if you throw it away once it'll never come your way again."

"No, I know," said Juliet, resting her arm on the mantelpiece, gravely watching him. "I've noticed that."

"Noticed it, have you?" He flung her a look as he passed. "You've never been in love, that's certain, never seriously. I mean—never up to the neck."

"No, never so deep as that!" replied Juliet.

He walked to the end of the room and came to a sudden stand before the window.

"I have," he said, and his voice came with an odd

jerkiness, as if it covered some emotion that he could not wholly control.

"I won't bore you with the details. But I loved a woman once—I loved her madly. And she loved me. But Fate came between. She's dead now.

"I sometimes think to myself that if I'd married that woman, I'd have made her happy, and I'd have been a better man myself than I am today."

He swung round restlessly, found her steady eyes upon him, and came back to her.

"The fact of the matter is, Miss Moore, I was a skunk ever to marry at all after that."

"It depends on how you look at it," she said gently.

"Don't you look at it that way?" he asked, regarding her curiously.

She hesitated momentarily.

"Not entirely, no. The woman was dead and you were alone."

"I was horribly alone."

"I don't think it was wrong of you to marry," she responded. "Only, you ought to love your wife."

"Ah! I thought we agreed that love comes only once."

She shook her head.

"Not quite that. Besides, there are many kinds of love."

Again for a second she hesitated, looking straight at him.

"Shall I tell you something? I don't know whether I ought. It is almost like a breach of confidence ... though it was never told to me."

"What is it?" he said imperatively.

She made a little gesture of yielding.

"Yes, I will tell you. Mr. Fielding, you might make your wife love you ... so dearly ... if you cared to take the trouble."

"What?"

Her eyes met his with a faint, faint smile.

"Doesn't it seem absurd that it should fall to me ... a comparative stranger ... to tell you this, when you have been together for so long? It is the truth. She is just as lonely and unhappy as you are. You could transform the whole world for her ... if you only would."

He stared at her for some seconds, as if trying to read some riddle in her countenance.

"You are a very remarkable young woman," he said at last. "So you think I might turn that very unreasonable hatred of hers into love, do you?"

"I am quite sure."

"I wonder if I should like it if I did!"

She laughed a sudden, low laugh.

"Yes, you would like it very much. It's the last and greatest obstacle between you and your happiness. Once clear that, and . . ."

"Did you say happiness?" he broke in cynically.

"Yes, of course I did." Her look challenged him. "Once clear that, and if you haven't got a straight run before you . . ."

She paused, looking at him oddly, very intently, and finally she stopped.

"Well?" he said. "Continue!"

She coloured vividly under his eyes.

"I'm afraid I've lost my thread. It doesn't really matter. You know what I was going to say. The way to happiness does not lie in pleasing oneself. The self-seekers never get there."

He made her a courteous bow.

"Thank you, fairy-godmother! I believe you are right. That may be why happiness is so shy a bird. We spread the net too openly.

"Well," he heaved a sigh, "we live and learn. How would you like to go over and see the cricket at Fairharbour this afternoon?"

"To be honest, I would rather . . . much . . . go to the open-air concert at High Shale this evening."

"Along with those rowdy miners?" growled the Squire. "I see enough of them on the Bench. Green, of course, is cracked on that subject. He'd like to set the world in order if he could."

"I admire his enterprise," said Juliet.

He nodded.

"So do I. He's cussed as a mule, but he's a goer. He's also a gentleman. Have you noticed that?"

She smiled.

"Of course I have."

"And I can't get my wife to see it. Just because—by

his own idiotic choice—he occupies a humble position, she won't allow him a single decent quality."

He moved restlessly.

"I would have placed him in his proper sphere if he'd consented to it. But he wouldn't. It's a standing grievance between us. That fellow Robin is a millstone round his neck."

He turned on her suddenly.

"You have a wonderful knack of making people see reason. Couldn't you persuade him to let Robin go?"

"Oh, no!" said Juliet quickly. "It's the very last thing I would attempt to do."

He looked at her in genuine astonishment.

Juliet flushed.

"But of course," she continued. "They belong to each other. How could Mr. Green possibly part with him? You wouldn't . . . surely . . . think much of him if he did?"

"I think he's mad not to," declared the Squire. "But I think it's uncommonly kind of you to take that view, all the same. I'll take you to that concert tonight if you really want to go."

"Will you? How kind," said Juliet, turning to go. "But you won't mind if I consult Mrs. Fielding first? I must do that."

He opened the door for her.

"You are not to spoil her now. She's been spoilt all her life by everybody."

"Except by you," replied Juliet daringly.

And with that parting shot she left him, swiftly traversing the Hall to the stairs without looking back.

The Squire stood for some seconds looking after her. She had opposed him at practically every point, and yet she had not offended him.

"A very remarkable young woman!" he said again to himself as she passed out of his sight. "A very gifted young woman! Ah, Dick my friend, she'd make a rare politician's wife."

And then another thought struck him, and he began to laugh.

"And she'd be equally charming as the helpmeet of the village Schoolmaster. Egad, we can't have everything, but I think you've found your fate."

*   *   *

Juliet drove off with the Squire on the way to the open-air concert on the High Shale bluff that evening.

Mrs. Fielding was too weary after the many emotions of the day to accompany them, but they left her in a tranquil frame of mind, and the Squire was in an unusually good humour.

Though he had small liking for the High Shale village people, it pleased him that Juliet should take an interest in Richard Green's enterprises, eccentric though they might be.

They neared their destination at last, and Jack performed what the Squire called his favourite circus trick—racing the car to the top of the towering cliff and stopping dead at the edge of a great immensity of sea and stars.

Juliet drew a deep breath of sheer marvelling delight, speaking no word, held spellbound by the wonder of the night.

"We needn't hurry," the Squire said. "They won't be starting yet."

So for a space they remained as though caught between earth and heaven, silently drinking in the splendour.

After a long pause she spoke.

"Do you often come here?"

"Not now. I used to in the days of my youth—the long-past days."

And she knew by his tone, by the lingering of his words, that he had not always come alone.

She asked no more, and presently the jaunty notes of a banjo floating up the grassy slope told them that Richard Green's entertainment had begun.

They left the car at the top of the rise and walked down over the springy turf towards the old barn about which Dick's audience were collected.

Two hurricane-lamps and a rough deal table were all he had in the way of stage property. But she was yet to learn that this man relied upon surroundings and circumstances not at all.

He sat on the edge of the deal table with one leg crossed over his knee, his dark face thrown into strong relief, intent, eager, with a vitality that seemed to make it almost luminous. From the crowd that watched him there came not a sound.

When the music ended a fisherman came forward and danced a hornpipe on the table, again to the thrumming of the banjo, without which nothing seemed complete.

The evening wore on, and with unfaltering resource Richard Green kept the interest of his audience from flagging.

He took something from his pocket; what it was Juliet could not see, but she caught the gleam of metal in the lamplight, and in a moment a great buzz of pleasure spread through the crowd.

And then it began, such music as she had never dreamt of, such music as surely was never fluted save from the pipes of Pan.

And it was to her alone that that wonder-music spoke. She and he were wandering alone together along that fairy-shore where every sea-shell gleamed like pearl and every wave broke iridescent at their feet.

The sun shone in the sky for them alone, and the caves were mystic palaces of delight that awaited their coming. And once it seemed to her that he drew her close, and she felt his kisses on her lips. . . .

Ah, surely this was the midsummer madness of which they had spoken! It was a vision that could not last, but the wonder of it she would carry forever in her heart.

It ended at last, but so softly, so tenderly, that, spellbound, she never knew when lingering sound became enduring silence.

She awoke as it were from a long dream and knew that her heart was beating with a wild and poignant longing that was pain. Then there arose a great shouting, and instinctively she laid her hand on the Squire's arm and drew him away.

"Had enough?" he asked.

She nodded. Somehow for the moment she could find no words. She had a feeling as of unshed tears at her throat. Ah, what had moved him to play to her like that? And why did it hurt her so?

She was thankful to be swooping back again through the summer night. An urgent desire for solitude was upon her. All her throbbing pulses cried out for it.

Later, alone in her room at the Court, she leant from

her open window, seeking with an almost frantic intensity to recover the peace that had been hers. How had she lost it? She could not say.

It had happened so suddenly, so amazingly. Yesterday she had been free. Perhaps even then the net had been about her feet, and he had known it. How otherwise had he spoken so intimately, dared so much?

She drew a long, deep breath, recalling his look, his touch, his voice.

Ah! Midsummer madness indeed! But she could not stay to face it. She must go. The way was still open behind her. She would escape as she had come, a fugitive from the force that pursued her so relentlessly.

She would not suffer herself to be made a captive. She would go.

Again she drew a long breath, but curiously it broke, as if a sharp spasm had gripped her heart. She stood, struggling with herself.

And then suddenly she dropped upon her knees by the sill, with her arms flung wide and her head with its cloudy mass of hair bowed low.

"O God! O God!" she whispered convulsively. "Save me from this! Help me to go . . . while I can! I am so tired . . . so tired!"

*   *   *

Columbus was not accustomed to being awakened in the early June morning and taken for a scamper when the sun was still scarcely two hours up. But Juliet was insistent.

"I'm going down to the shore, you old sleepy-head," she told him. "Don't you want to come?"

She herself had scarcely slept throughout the brief night, and a great yearning for the sunshine and the sea was upon her. The solitude of the beach drew her irresistibly.

It was Sunday morning and she knew that no-one but herself would be up for hours.

She had grown to love it so, the silence and the shining emptiness and the marvel of the sea. She could not remember any other place that had ever attracted her in the same way. It suited every mood.

She reached the shingly shore and went down over the stones to the waves breaking in the sunlight. Yes, she was tired, she was tired; but this was peace.

She sat down and put her arms round her faithful companion and leant her head against his rough coat.

The tide was coming in. The white-lipped waves broke in flashing foam that spread almost to her feet. The sparkle of it danced in her dreaming eyes, but it did not rouse her from her reverie.

Perhaps she was half-asleep after the weary watching of the night, or perhaps she was only too tired to notice, but when a voice suddenly spoke behind her she started as if at an electric shock.

"Are you waiting for the sea to carry you away?" the voice said. "Because you won't have to wait much longer now."

She turned as she sat. She had heard no sound of approaching feet. She looked up at him with a feeling of utter helplessness.

"You!" she said.

He stood behind her, slim, upright, intensely vital, in the morning light. She had an impression that he was dressed in loose flannels, and she saw a bath-towel hanging round his neck.

"You have been bathing."

He laughed down at her; she saw the gleam of the white teeth in his dark face.

"I say, what a good guess! You look shocked. Is it wrong to bathe on Sunday?"

And then quite naturally he stretched a hand to her and helped her to her feet.

"I've been watching you for a long time," he said. "I was only a dot in the ocean, so of course you didn't see me. I say—tell me—what's the matter?"

The question was so sudden that it caught her unawares. She found herself looking straight into the dark eyes and wondering at their steady kindliness.

She knew instinctively that she looked into the eyes of a friend, so it was as a friend she spoke in answer.

"I have had rather a worrying night. I came out for a little fresh air. It was such a perfect morning."

"And you hoped you would have the place to yourself and be able to cry it off in comfort. I wouldn't have interfered if I hadn't been afraid that you were going to drown yourself in the bargain. And I really couldn't bear that."

She laughed a little in spite of herself.

"No, I have no intention of drowning myself. I am not so desperate as that."

He smiled at her whimsically.

"It happens sometimes unintentionally. Let's climb up to the next shelf and sit down!"

Her hand was still in his. He kept it to help her up the tumbling stones to a higher ridge of shingle.

"Will this do?" he asked her. "May I stay for a bit? I'll be very good."

"You always are good," replied Juliet as she sat down.

"No? Really? You don't mean that? Well, it's awfully kind of you if you do, but it isn't true."

He dropped down beside her.

"I have been a devil sometimes."

"Yes, I know."

"Oh, you know that, do you? How do you know?"

He was watching her closely, but as the faint colour mounted to her face, his eyes fell.

"No, don't tell me! It doesn't matter."

They sat in silence for a while, then he spoke again.

"Juliet," he said, his voice very low, "am I being a nuisance to you?"

She looked at him swiftly. He had uttered the name so spontaneously that she wondered if he realised that he had made use of it.

Before she could find words to answer him, he went on:

"I'm not a bounder. At least I hope not. But yesterday—last night—I hadn't got such a firm hold on myself as usual.

"Then when I knew you were standing there listening, temptation came to me, and I hadn't the strength to resist. You knew, didn't you? You understood?"

She nodded mutely.

"Will you forgive me?" he asked.

She was silent. How could she tell him what that wild passion of music had done to her?

"I hope you'll try, anyway," he went on after a

moment, "because I never meant to offend you. Only somehow I felt possessed. I had to reach you or die. But I didn't mean to hurt you."

His voice was still very low, but it had steadied.

"My dear, you do believe that, don't you? My love is more than a selfish craving. I can do without you. I will—since I must. But I shall go on loving you—all my life."

And suddenly the hot tears welled up in Juliet's eyes. She could not speak in answer, but in a moment she stretched out her hand to his.

He took it and held it close.

"Don't cry," he said gently. "I'm not worth it. I've been a fool—no, not a fool to love you, but a three-times idiot to lose hold of myself like this. You're not going to run away because of me, are you? Promise you won't?"

Her fingers closed upon his. It was almost involuntary.

"I don't think I ought to stay," she whispered.

"I knew it was that!" He bent towards her. "Juliet! If one of us must go, it must be I. But there is no need. I won't come near you—I swear—if you don't wish it."

"Oh, stop!" Juliet said, and suddenly her face was turned upwards on his shoulder and her forehead was against his neck. "You're making the biggest mistake of your life!"

"What?" he said, and fell abruptly silent and so tensely still that she thought even his heart must have been arrested on the word.

The colour rushed in vivid scarlet to her temples. She met his eyes for one fleeting second, then closed her own with a gasp and a blind effort to escape, which was instantly quelled.

For he kissed her—he kissed her—pressing his lips to hers closely and ever more closely, as a man consumed with thirst draining the cup to the last precious drop.

When he let her go, she was burning, quivering, tingling from head to foot as if an electric current were coursing through and through her.

But he did not kiss her a second time. He only held her against his heart.

"Ah, Juliet—Juliet!"

As he uttered the words, she felt the deep quiver in his voice.

"I've got you—now! You are mine."

She was panting, wordless, thankful to avail herself of the shelter he offered. She leant against him for many seconds in palpitating silence.

For so long indeed was she silent that in the end misgiving pierced him, and he felt for the downcast face. But in a moment she reached up and took his hand in hers, restraining him.

"Not again!" she whispered. "Please, not again!"

"All right. I won't," he replied. "Not yet, anyhow. But speak to me! Tell me it's all right! You're not frightened?"

She shook her head, then lifted the hand she had taken and laid it against her cheek.

"I've got . . . a good deal to say to you, Dick. You've taken me so completely by storm. Please be generous now! Please let me have the honours of war!"

"My darling!"

He let her go with the words, and she clasped her hands about her knees and looked out to sea. She was still trembling a little, but as he sat beside her in unbroken silence she grew gradually calmer, and presently she spoke without any apparent difficulty.

"You've taken a good deal for granted, Dick, haven't you? You don't know me very well."

"Don't I?"

"No. You've been dreadfully headlong all through." She smiled faintly, with a touch of sadness. "You've skipped all the usual preliminaries . . . which isn't always wise. Don't you teach your boys to look before they leap?"

"When there's time," he replied, "but you know, you gave the word for the final plunge."

She nodded slowly once or twice.

"Yes. But the fact remains, we haven't known each other long."

She made a little movement towards him but she did not turn.

"I don't want to hurt you. But I'm going to ask of you something that you won't like at all."

"Well, what is it?" he asked.

"I want you," she paused, then turned and resolutely faced him, "I want you to be . . . just friends with me again."

"For how long?"

Swiftly he asked the question, his eyes still holding hers with a certain mastery of possession.

She made a slight gesture of pleading.

"Until you know me better."

His brows went up.

"You don't really expect me to agree to that. Now do you?"

"Ah! But you've got to understand, I'm not in the least the sort of woman you think. I'm not . . . Dick, I'm not . . . a specially good woman."

She spoke the words with painful effort, her eyes wavering before his.

"My darling, don't tell me that! I can see what you are. It's you that I love—just as you are. If you were one atom less human, you wouldn't be you, and my love—our love—might never have been."

She was silent, but her look was dubious. He drew suddenly close to her and slipped his hand through her arm.

"Is there anything else that really matters at all? Juliet, tell me! I've got to know. Does—Robin matter?"

She started at the question. It was obviously unexpected.

"No! Of course not!"

"Thank you," he said steadily. "I loved you for that before you said it."

She laid her hand upon his and held it.

"That's one of the things I love you for, Dick," she said, with eyes downcast. "You are so . . . splendidly . . . loyal."

"Sweetheart!" He spoke softly. "There's no virtue in that."

Her brows were slightly drawn.

"I think there is. Anyway, it appeals to me tremendously. You would stick to Robin . . . whatever the cost."

"Well, that—of course. I flatter myself I am necessary to Robin. But with Jack it is otherwise. I've kicked him out."

"Dick!"

She looked at him in sharp amazement.

He smiled a thin-lipped smile.

"Yes. It had to be. I've put up with him long enough. I told him so last night."

"You quarrelled?"

"No. We didn't quarrel. I gave him his marching orders, that's all."

"But wasn't he very angry?"

"Oh, pshaw! What of it?"

She was looking at him intently, for there was something merciless about his smile.

"Do you always do that, I wonder," she questioned, "with the people who make you angry?"

"Do what?"

"Kick them out." Her voice held a doubtful note.

He turned his hand upwards and clasped hers.

"My darling, it was a perfectly just sentence. He deserved it. He can make his own way in life. It's high time he did. I didn't kick him out because I was angry with him either."

"But you were angry," she persisted. "You were nearly white-hot."

He laughed.

"I kept my hands off him, anyhow. But never mind that now! You don't regard Robin as a just cause and impediment. What's the next obstacle? My profession?"

"No," she said instantly and emphatically. "I like that part of you. There's something rather quaint about it."

His quick smile flashed upon her, and she coloured slightly.

"It doesn't really count one way or the other with me, Dick, any more than it would count with you. It's only . . ."

She hesitated.

"Go on!" he commanded.

"And if I can't tell you, Dick? If . . . if it's just an instinct that says, Wait? We've been too headlong as it is. I can't . . . I daren't . . . go on at this pace."

She was almost tearful.

"I must have a little breathing-space. I came here for peace and quietness, as you know."

He broke into a sudden laugh.

"So you did. You were playing hide-and-seek with yourself, weren't you? I'll bet you never expected to find the other half of yourself in this remote corner, did you?"

His eyes gleamed.

"Well, never mind! Don't cry, sweetheart—anyhow not till you've got a decent excuse! I don't want to rush you into anything against your will. But we must have things on a sensible footing. You see that, don't you?"

"If we could just be friends."

"Well, I'm quite willing to be friends." He laughed into her eyes. "Why so distressful? Don't you like the prospect?"

She drew his hand down into her lap and held it between her own, looking gravely down at it.

"Dick!" she said.

His smile passed.

"What is it? You're not going to be afraid of me?"

"I want you to leave me free a little longer," she answered.

"Until you are ready to marry me," he suggested quietly.

A quick tremor went through her.

"That won't be for a long time."

"How long?"

"I don't know, Dick. I haven't the least idea."

"All right," he said unexpectedly. "But facts are facts. We may not be engaged, but we are—permanently— attached. We'll leave it at that."

Again she glanced swiftly towards him.

"No, but, Dick . . ."

"Yes, but, Juliet . . ."

His hand moved suddenly, imprisoning both of hers.

"You can't get away," he went on, speaking very rapidly, "any more than I can."

She quivered at his words.

"If you put the whole world between us," he went on, "we shall still belong to each other. That is irrevocable. It isn't your doing, and it isn't mine. It's a power above and beyond us both. We can't help ourselves."

He spoke with fierce earnestness, a depth of concentration, that gripped her just as his music had gripped her the night before.

She sat motionless, bound by the same spell that had bound her then. She did not want to meet his eyes, but they drew her irresistibly. In the end she did so.

She spoke at last, her eyes still held by his.

"I think you are right. We can't help it. But, oh, Dick, remember that ... remember that ... if ever there should come a time when you wish you had done ... otherwise!"

"If ever I do what? Do you mind saying that again?"

She shook her head.

"But I'm not laughing. Dick. You've carried me out of my depth, and ... I'm not a very good swimmer."

"All right, darling," he said. "Lean on me! I'll hold you up."

She clasped his hand tightly.

"You will be patient?"

He smiled into her face.

"As patient as patient! That means I'm not to tell anybody, does it?"

She bent her head.

"Yes, Dick."

"All right," he conceded. "I won't tell a soul without your consent. But . . ."

He leant nearer to her, speaking almost under his breath.

"When I am alone with you, Juliet—I shall take you in my arms—and kiss you—as I have done today."

Again a swift tremor went through her. She looked at him no longer.

"Oh, but not ... not without my leave," she whispered.

"You will give me leave!"

"I believe you could make me give you anything."

"But you can't give me what is mine already," he answered quietly, as he pressed the two trembling hands against his heart. "That is understood, isn't it? And when you are tired of working for your living, you will come to me and let me work for you."

She made a little movement as if she would free herself, but checked it on the instant. Then very slowly she lifted her face to his, but she did not meet his look. Her eyes were closed.

"Someday," she said with quivering lips, "someday
... I will."

He took her face between his hands and held it as if
he waited for something.

"Someday—wife of my heart!" he murmured very
softly, and kissed the eyes that would not meet his own.

Chapter
Five

The annual flower-show at Fairharbour was one of the chief events of the district, and entailed such a gathering of the county as Vera Fielding would not for worlds have missed.

Juliet herself would gladly have stayed away, but Mrs. Fielding would not hear of leaving her behind.

As Dick had predicted, she had come to lean upon Juliet, and her dependence became every day more pronounced.

It was not an easy position, but Juliet filled it to the best of her ability and with no small self-sacrifice.

Yet in a sense it made her life the simpler, for she was still at that difficult stage when it is easier to stand still than to go forward.

She saw Dick when he came to the house, but they had not been alone together since the morning on the shore when her love had betrayed her.

She had a feeling that he was biding his time. He had promised to be patient, and she knew he would keep his promise.

Also, his time, like hers, was very fully occupied, and in her secret soul Juliet was thankful that this was so. For the present it was enough for her to hold this new joy close, close to her heart, to gaze upon it only in solitude.

It was a gift most precious, upon which no other eyes might look.

It was enough for her to feel the tight grasp of his hand when they met, to catch for an instant the quick

gleam of understanding in his glance, the sudden flash of
that smile which was for her alone.

She was absurdly, superbly happy.

"I believe this place suits you," the Squire said to her
once. "You look years younger than when you came."

She received the compliment with her low, soft
laugh.

He gave her a sharp look.

"You are happy here? Not sorry you came?"

"Oh, not in the least sorry."

He nodded.

"That's all right. You've done Vera a lot of good."

He was on his way out of the room, but a sudden
thought seemed to strike him and he lingered.

"Shall I make Green come to the flower-show with
us?" he asked.

"I shouldn't," said Juliet quietly. "He probably
wouldn't have time, and certainly Mrs. Fielding wouldn't
want him."

He frowned.

"Would you like him?" he asked abruptly.

"I?"

She met his look with a baffling smile.

"Oh, don't ask him on my account! I am quite happy
without a cavalier in attendance."

The Squire went out looking extremely dissatisfied.
But when the day arrived and they were on the point of
departure he surprised them both by the sudden an-
nouncement that Richard Green was to be picked up at
the gates. It was a Saturday afternoon, and for once he
was at liberty.

"Oh, really, Edward!" Mrs. Fielding protested. "Now
you've spoilt everything."

Juliet saw the Squire's mouth take an ominous down-
ward curve, but to her relief he kept his temper in check.
He was driving the car himself, which was an open one.
Somewhat grimly he turned to Juliet.

"I hope you have no objection to sharing the back-
seat with Mr. Green?"

She felt her pulses give a swift leap at the question,
but with a hasty effort she kept down her rising colour.

"Of course not!" she replied.

They shot down the avenue at a speed that brought them very rapidly in sight of the gates. A figure was waiting there, and again Juliet was conscious of the hard beating of her heart.

Richard Green came forward, greeted the Squire and Mrs. Fielding, and in a moment was getting in beside her.

"Good-afternoon, Miss Moore!" he said.

She gave him her hand and felt his fingers close with a spring-like strength upon it, while his eyes laughed into hers. Then the car was in motion again, and he dropped into the seat.

It was barely half-an-hour's run to Burchester Park, which was thrown open to the public for the great occasion. The Castle also was open on that day, and visitors were arriving from every quarter.

The Squire ran the car into a deep patch of shade beside the road and stopped.

"We had better get out here," he said, "and we'll do the flower-show first."

They entered the first sweltering tent, and in the throng she felt again the touch of Dick's hand as he followed behind.

"We mustn't lose each other," he said with a laugh.

The midsummer madness was upon her, and, without looking at him, she squeezed the fingers that gripped her arm.

"Look here," he whispered in her ear, "let's get away! Let's get lost! It's the easiest thing in the world. We can't all hang together in this crowd."

This was quite evident. The great marquee was crammed with people, and already the Squire was piloting his wife to the opening at the other end.

"We must just look round," murmured Juliet, "for decency's sake."

"Haven't you had enough of it?" he asked after several minutes. "Let us go!"

She turned obediently from a glorious spread of gloxinias, and he made a way for her through the buzzing crowd to the entrance. When Dick spoke with the voice of authority, it was her pleasure to submit.

She felt her pulses tingle as she followed him, to be alone with him again, to feel herself encompassed by the fiery magic of his love, to yield throbbing surrender to the mastery that would not be denied.

"That's better," he said, drawing a deep breath. "Now we can get away."

"We shan't get away from the people."

He threw a rapid glance round.

"Yes, we shall—with any luck. There's a little landing-stage place down by the lake. We'll go there. There may even be a boat handy—if the gods are kind."

They skirted the terraced gardens, which were not open to the public, and plunged down a winding walk through a shrubbery that led somewhat sharply downwards.

Away from the noise and the crush into cool green depths of woodland, through which at last there shone up at them the gleam of water.

Juliet caught sight of a white skiff in the water close to the bank. The final descent was a decided scramble, but he held her up until the mossy bank was reached; and would have held her longer, but with a little breathless laugh she released herself.

"My shoes are ruined," she remarked.

"I say, they are wet through! You must take them off at once. Get into the boat!"

"Do you think we ought to get into that boat? Suppose the owner comes along?"

"The owner? Lord Saltash, do you mean?" He scoffed at the idea. "No, he is probably many salt-miles away in that ocean-going yacht of his. Lucky dog!"

"Oh, do you envy him?"

He gave her a shrewd glance.

"Not in the least. He is welcome to his yacht, and his Lady Jo, and all that is his."

"Dick!" She made a swift gesture of repudiation. "Please don't repeat that . . . scandal . . . again!"

He raised his brows with a faintly ironic smile.

"Are you still giving her the benefit of the doubt? I imagine no-one else does."

The colour went out of her face. She stood quite motionlessly, looking not at him but at a whirl of dancing gnats on the gold-flecked water beyond him.

"She went to Paris," she said, in the tone of one asserting a fact that no-one could dispute.

"So did he. The yacht went round to Bordeaux to pick him up afterwards. I understand that he was not alone."

She turned on him in sudden anger.

"Why do you repeat this horrible gossip? Where do you hear it?"

He held out his hand to her.

"Juliet, I repeat it because I want you to know—you have got to know—that she is unworthy of your friendship."

He spoke without anger but with a force and authority that carried far more weight.

"Juliet, you have always known her for a heartless flirt. You broke with her because she jilted the man she was about to marry. Now that she has gone to another man, surely you have done with her!"

Juliet's indignation passed at his words, but she did not touch his outstretched hand, and in a moment he bent and took hers.

"Now I've made you furious," he said.

She looked at him somewhat piteously, essaying a smile with lips that trembled.

"No, I am not furious. Only ... when you talk like that you make me ... rather uneasy. You see, Lady Jo and I have always been ... birds of a feather."

"Don't! I can't have you talk like that—couple yourself with that woman whose main amusement for years has been to break as many hearts as she could capture."

He gripped her hand so hard that she almost gasped in pain.

"Forget her, darling," he went on. "Promise me you will. Come! We're not going to let her spoil this perfect day."

He was drawing her to him, but she sought to resist him, and even when his arms were close about her she did not wholly yield. He held her to him, but he did not press for a full surrender.

And, perhaps because of his forbearance, she presently lifted her face to his and clung to him with all her quivering strength.

"Just for today, Dick!" she whispered tremulously. "Just for today!"

Their lips met upon the words.

"Forever and ever!" he answered passionately as he held her to his heart.

*   *   *

The sunshine was no less bright or the day less full of summer warmth when they floated out upon the lake a little later. But Juliet's mood had changed.

She leant back on Dick's coat in the stern of the boat, drifting her fingers through the rippling water with a thoughtful face.

They reached the middle of the lake, and Dick let his sculls rest upon the water, sending feathery splashes from their tips that spread in widening circles all round them.

As if in answer to an unspoken word, Juliet's eyes came up to his. She faintly smiled.

"Have you brought that woodland pipe of yours?"

He smiled back at her.

"No. I am keeping that for another occasion."

She lifted her straight brows interrogatively, without speaking.

He answered her, still smiling, but with that in his voice that brought the warm colour to her face:

"For the day when we go away together, sweetheart, and don't come back."

Her eyes sank before his, but in a moment or two she lifted them again, meeting his look with something of an effort.

"I wonder, Dick," she said slowly, "I wonder if we ever shall."

He leant towards her.

"Are you daring me to run away with you?"

She shook her head.

"I should probably turn into something very hideous if you did, and that would be . . . rather terrible for both of us."

"That's a parable, is it?"

He was still looking at her keenly, earnestly.

She made a little gesture of remonstrance, as if his regard were too much for her.

"You can take it as you please. But as I have no intention of running away with you, perhaps it is beside the point."

He laughed with a hint of mastery.

"Our intentions on that subject may not be the same. I'll back mine against yours any day."

She smiled at his words, though her colour mounted higher. After a moment she sat up and laid a hand upon his knee.

"Dick, you're getting too managing ... much. I suppose it's the Schoolmaster part of you."

His hand was on hers in an instant; she thrilled to the electricity of his touch.

"No—no! That's just the soul of me, darling, leaping all the obstacles to reach and hold you. You're not going to tell me you have no use for that?"

"But you promised to be patient."

"Well, I will be. I am. Don't look so serious! What have I done?"

His eyes challenged her to laughter, and she laughed, though somewhat uncertainly.

"Nothing ... yet, Dick. But I don't feel at all sure of you today. I haven't the least idea what you will do next."

"What a mercy I've got you safe in the boat!" he said. "I didn't know you were so shy. What shall I do to reassure you?"

His hand moved up her wrist with the words, softly pushing up the lacy sleeve, till it found the bend of the elbow, and he stooped and kissed the delicate blue veins, closely, with lips that lingered.

Then, his head still bent low, very tenderly he spoke.

"Don't be afraid of my love, sweetheart! Let it be your defence!"

She was sitting very still in his hold, save that every fibre of her throbbed at the touch off his lips. But in a moment she moved, touched his shoulder, his neck, with fingers that trembled, and finally she smoothed the close black hair.

"Why did you make me love you?" she asked, and uttered a sharp sigh that caught her unawares.

He laughed as he raised his head.

"Poor darling! You didn't want to, did you? I believe it's upset all your plans for the future."

"It has," she replied. "At least it threatens to!"

"What a shame!" He spoke commiseratingly. "And

what were your plans—if it isn't impertinent of me to ask that question?"

She smiled faintly.

"Well, marriage certainly wasn't one of them. And I'm not sure that it is now. I feel like the girl in *Marionettes*, Cynthia Paramount, who said she didn't think any woman ought to marry until she had been engaged at least six times."

Dick sat up suddenly and returned to his sculls.

"Juliet, why did you read that book? I told you not to."

Her smile deepened, though her eyes were grave. She clasped her fingers about her knees.

"My dear Dick, that's why. It didn't hurt me like *The Valley of Dry Bones*. In fact, I was feeling so nice and superior when I read it that I rather enjoyed it."

Dick sent the boat through the water with a long stroke. His face was stern. After a moment Juliet looked at him.

"Are you cross with me because I read it, Dick?"

His face softened instantly.

"With you! What an idea!"

"With the man who wrote it then?" she suggested. "He exasperates me intensely. He has such a maddeningly clear vision, and he is so inevitably right."

"And yet you persist in reading him?" Dick's voice had a faintly mocking note.

"And yet I persist in reading him. You see, I am a woman, Dick. I haven't your lordly faculty for ignoring the people I most dislike. I detest Dene Strange, but I can't overlook him. No-one can. I think his character-studies are quite marvellous."

She frowned throughtfully.

"That girl and her endless flirtations, and then . . . when the real thing came to her at last . . . that unspeakable man of iron refusing to take her because she had jilted another man, ruining both their lives for the sake of his own rigid code!"

Her voice hardened.

"He didn't deserve her in any case. She was too good for him, with all her faults."

Juliet paused, studying her lover's face attentively.

"I hope you're not that sort of man, Dick."

He met her eyes.

"Why do you say that?"

"Because there's a high-priestly expression about your mouth that rather looks as if you might be. Please don't tell me if you are, because it will spoil all my pleasure."

"Juliet, though I wouldn't spoil your pleasure for the world, I must say one thing."

His voice became resolute.

"If a woman engages herself to a man, I consider that she is bound in honour to fulfil her engagement—unless he sets her free. I hold that sort of engagement to be a debt of honour—as sacred as the marriage-vow itself."

"Even though she realises that she is going to make a mistake?"

"Whatever the circumstances," he continued. "An engagement can only be broken by mutual consent. Otherwise, the very word becomes a farce. I have no sympathy with jilts of either sex."

Juliet looked up with a smile.

"I think you and Dene Strange ought to collaborate. You would soon put this naughty world to rights between you."

There was in her tone, despite its playfulness, a delicate finality that told him plainly that she had no intention of pursuing the subject further, and, curiously, the man's heart smote him for a moment.

He felt as if in some fashion wholly inexplicable he had hurt her.

"You're not cross with me, sweetheart?"

She looked at him, still smiling, but her look and her smile were more of a veil than a revelation.

"With you! What an idea!" she answered, softly mocking.

"Ah, don't! I'm not like that, Juliet!"

"Ah, Dick! Don't . . . don't upset the boat!"

For the sculls floated loose again in the row-locks. He had her by the wrists, the arms, the shoulders. He had her, suddenly and very closely, against his heart. He covered her face with his kisses, so that she gasped and gasped for breath, half-laughing, half-dismayed.

"Dick, how . . . how disgraceful of you! Dick, you mustn't! Someone . . . someone will see us!"

"Let them!" he replied, grimly reckless. "You brought

it on yourself. How dare you tell me I'm like a high priest? How dare you, Juliet?"

"I daren't," she assured him, her hand against his mouth, restraining him. "I never will again. Please be good! I am sure someone is watching us. I can feel it in my bones. Please, Dick . . . darling . . . please!"

He held the appealing hand and kissed it very tenderly.

"I can't resist that. So now we're quits, are we? And no-one any the worse. Juliet, you'll have to marry me soon."

She drew away from his arms, still panting a little. Her face was burning.

"Now we'll go back. You're very unmanageable today. I shall not come out with you again for a long time."

"Yes—yes you will," he urged. "I shouldn't be so unmanageable if I weren't so starved."

She laughed rather shakily.

"You're absurd and extravagant. Please row back now, Dick! Mr. and Mrs. Fielding will be wondering where we are."

"Let 'em wonder!" said Dick.

Nevertheless, moved by something in her voice or her face, he turned the boat and began to row back to the shore.

He pulled quickly with swift strokes, and presently the skiff glided up to the little landing-stage. He shipped the sculls and held to the woodwork with one hand.

"Will you get ashore, darling, and I'll tie up. There's no-one here to see."

"No-one that matters," said a laughing voice above him, and suddenly a man in a white yachting-suit, slim, dark, stepped out from the spreading shadow of a beech.

"Hullo!" exclaimed Dick, startled.

"Hullo, Sir! Delighted to meet you. Madam, will you take my hand? Ah—*et tu, Juliette!* Delighted to meet you also."

He was bowing, with one hand extended, the other on his heart. Juliet, still seated in the stern of the boat, had gone suddenly white to the lips.

She gasped a little, and in a moment forced a laugh that somehow sounded desperate.

"Why, it is Charles Rex!"

Dick's eyes came swiftly to her.

"Who? Lord Saltash, isn't it? I thought so." His look flashed back to the man above him with something of a challenge. "You know the lady, then?"

Two eyes looked down into his, answering the challenge with gay inconsequence.

"Sir, I have that inestimable privilege. *Juliette*, will you not accept my hand?"

Juliet's hand came upwards a little uncertainly; then, as he grasped it, she stood up in the boat.

"This is indeed a surprise. Rumour had it that you were a hundred miles away at least."

"Rumour!" Lord Saltash laughed. "How often has rumour played havoc with my name! Not an unpleasant surprise, I trust?"

He handed her ashore, laughing on a note of mockery. Charles Burchester, Lord Saltash, said to be of Royal descent, possessed in no small degree the charm not untempered with wickedness of his reputed ancestor.

His friends had dubbed him "the merry monarch" long since, but to Juliet he had been Charles Rex from the day she had first bestowed the title upon him. Somehow, in all his varying—sometimes amazing—moods, it suited him.

She stood with him on the little wooden landing-stage, her hand still in his, and the colour coming back into her face.

"But of course not!" she said in answer to his light words, laughing still a trifle breathlessly. "If you will promise not to prosecute us for trespassing!"

"*Mais, Juliette!*" He bent over her hand. "You could not trespass if you tried. And the cavalier with you—may I not have the honour of an introduction?"

He knew how to jest with grace in an awkward moment. Dick realised that as, having secured the boat, he presented himself for Juliet's low-spoken introduction.

"Mr. Green . . . Lord Saltash!"

Lord Saltash extended a hand, his eyes full of quizzical amusement.

"I've heard your name before, I think. And I believe I've seen you somewhere too. Ah, yes! It's coming back!"

He smiled.

"You are the Orpheus who plays the flute to the wild
beasts at High Shale. I've been wanting to meet you.
listened to you from my car one night, and—on my soul—
I nearly wept."

Dick smiled with a touch of cynicism.

"Miss Moore was listening that night, too."

"Yes," Juliet said quickly. "I was there."

Lord Saltash looked at her questioningly for a moment, then his look returned to Dick.

"I am the friend who never tells," he observed. "So it
was Miss Moore you were playing to, was it? Ah, *Juliette!*"

He threw her a sudden smile.

"I wish I could play like that!"

She uttered her soft, low laugh.

"No, you have quite enough accomplishments, *mon
ami.* Now, if you don't mind, I think we had better walk
back and find Mr. and Mrs. Fielding. I am with them
. . . as Mrs. Fielding's Companion.

"I . . ." she hesitated momentarily, "have left Lady
Jo."

"Oh, I know that," Lord Saltash replied. "I've missed
you badly. We all have. When are you coming back to
us?"

"I don't know," Juliet replied.

"Rather hard on Lady Jo," he suggested. "Don't you
miss her at all?"

"No," answered Juliet. "I can't . . . honestly . . . say I
do."

"Oh, let us be honest at all costs!" he said. "Do you
know what Lady Jo is doing now?"

Juliet hesitated an instant, as if the subject were
distasteful to her.

"I can guess," she responded somewhat distantly and
coldly.

"I'll bet you can't," said Lord Saltash, with a twist of
the eyebrows that was oddly characteristic of him. "So I'll
tell you. She's running in an obstacle race, and—to be
quite, quite honest—I don't think she's going to win."

There was a moment's pause. Then the man on
Juliet's other side spoke, briefly and with decision.

"Miss Moore is no longer interested in Lady Joanna
Farringmore's doings. Their friendship is at an end."

Juliet made a slight gesture of remonstrance, but she spoke no word of contradiction.

A gleam of malice danced in Lord Saltash's eyes; it was like the turn of a rapier in a practised hand.

"Most wise and proper! *Juliette,* I always admired your discretion."

"You were always very kind, Charles Rex," she replied gravely.

*　　*　　*

They went back up the winding glen, and as they went Lord Saltash talked, superbly at his ease, of the doings of the past few weeks.

They reached the shrubbery to be nearly deafened by the band.

"Come through the gardens!" said Lord Saltash, with a shudder. "We must get out of this somehow."

"But the Fieldings," objected Juliet.

"Oh, Mr. Green will go and find them, won't you, Mr. Green?"

Saltash turned a disarming smile upon him.

But Dick looked straight back without a smile.

"Miss Moore is under my escort," he observed. "If she agrees, I think we had better go together."

"And do you agree, *Juliette?*" enquired Lord Saltash with interest.

Curiously, a spirit of perversity seemed to have entered into Juliet, and she looked directly at Dick.

"I wish you would go and find them. I know they will be wondering where we are."

His brows went up. She thought he was going to refuse. And then quite suddenly he yielded.

"Certainly, if you wish it. And when they are found?"

"Oh, dump them in the Great Hall!" replied Lord Saltash. "To be left till called for!"

"Charles!" protested Juliet.

He grinned at her, a wicked, monkeyish grin, and threw open the door, disclosing a steep and winding stone stair.

"That's a masterful sort of person," observed Lord Saltash, as they mounted the dimly lit turret stair. "What does he do for a living?"

Juliet hesitated, conscious of a strong repugnance to discuss her lover with this man from her old world.

But she could not withhold an answer to so ordinary a question. Moreover, Lord Saltash could be imperious when he chose, and she knew instinctively that it was not wise to cross him.

"By profession," she said slowly, "he is . . . a village Schoolmaster."

Lord Saltash's laugh stung, though it was exactly what she had expected. But he qualified it with careless generosity.

"Quite a presentable cavalier, *ma Juliette!* And a fixed occupation is something of an advantage at times. And how soon do you ride away? Or is that question premature?"

Juliet's face burnt in the dimness, but she was in front of him and was thankfully aware that he could not see it.

"I am not answering any more questions, Charles. Now that you have got me into your ogre's castle, you must be . . . kind."

"I will be kindness itself," he assured her. "You know I am the soul of hospitality. All I have is yours."

The narrow stair ended at a small stone landing on which was a door. Juliet stepped aside as she reached it, and waited for her host.

"It's rather like a prison."

"You won't think so when you get through the door," he replied. "By Jove! To think that I've actually got you—you of all people—here in my stronghold."

Then he turned abruptly and flung open the door against which he stood.

It led into a winding passage of such a totally different character from the stone staircase they had just mounted that Juliet stood gazing down it for some seconds before she obeyed his mute gesture to pass through.

It was thickly carpeted, deadening all sound, and the walls were hung with some heavy material the colour of old oak.

The passage ended in heavy curtains of the same dark brown material.

She stopped and looked at her companion.

"What is it?" he asked, with a laugh. "Are you afraid of my inner sanctuary?"

He parted the curtains, disclosing a tall oak door. She saw no latch upon it, but his hand went up behind the curtain, and she heard the click of a spring. In a moment the tall door opened before her.

"Go in!" he said easily.

She entered a strange room, oak-panelled, shaped like a cone, lighted only by a glass dome in the roof.

It was the most curious chamber she had ever seen. She trod on a tiger-skin as she entered, and noted that the floor was covered with them. There was no chair anywhere, only a long, deep couch, also draped with tiger-skins.

She heard the door click behind her and, turning, realised that it had disappeared in the oak panelling against which her host was standing.

He laughed at her quizzically.

"I believe you are frightened."

She looked round her, seeing no exit anywhere.

"It is just the sort of freak apartment I should expect you to delight in!" she exclaimed.

"You wouldn't have come if you had known, would you?" he said, a faint note of jeering in his voice.

She turned and faced him.

"Don't be ridiculous, Charles! You see, I happen to know you."

He looked at her.

"Why did you run away?"

She hesitated.

"That's a hard question, isn't it?"

"Oh, don't mind me! I don't flatter myself that I was the cause."

Her dark brows were slightly drawn.

"No, you were not. It was just . . . it was Lady Jo herself, Charlie. No-one else."

"Ah!" His goblin smile flashed out at her. "Poor, erring Lady Jo! Don't be too hard on her! She has her points."

She laid her hand quickly on his arm.

"Don't try to defend her! She is quite despicable. I have done with her."

His hand was instantly on hers. He laughed into her eyes.

"I'll wager you have a lingering fellow-feeling for her even yet."

"Not since she was reported to have run away with you," countered Juliet.

She turned to the deep settee and sank down among tiger-skins with a sigh.

He opened a cupboard in the panelling of the wall, and there followed the chink of glasses and the cheery buzz of a syphon. In a few moments he came to her with a tall glass in his hand containing a frothy drink.

"Look here, *Juliette!* Come to France with me on *The Night Moth* and we'll find Lady Jo!"

She accepted the drink and lay back without looking at him.

"No, never!" she replied firmly.

He leant down to her.

"I say you will. This is a midsummer madness. This will pass."

She started slightly at his words. The sparkling liquid splashed over. She lifted the glass to her lips and drank. When she ceased he took it softly from her and slipped his arm behind her.

"*Juliette*, I am going to save you from yourself."

She drew away from him.

"Charles, I forbid that!"

She was breathing quickly, but her voice was quiet. There was an indomitable resolution in her eyes.

He paused, looking at her closely.

"You deny—to me—what you were permitting with so much freedom barely half-an-hour ago to the village Schoolmaster?"

Her face flamed.

"I have always denied you that!"

He smiled.

"Times alter, *Juliette*. You are no longer in a position to deny me."

She kept her eyes upon him.

"You mean I have trusted you too far? I might have known!"

He shrugged his shoulders.

"Life is a game of hazard, is it not? And you were always a daring player. But you cannot always win. This time the luck is against you."

She was silent. Very slowly her eyes left his. She drooped forward as she sat.

He leant down to her again, his face oddly sympathetic.

"After all—you claimed my protection."

She made a sudden movement. She turned sharply, almost blindly. She caught him by the shoulders.

"Oh, Charles! Charles Rex! Is there no mercy . . . no honour . . . in you?"

He looked at her quizzically.

"Well, listen, *Juliette!* I'll strike a bargain with you. When you are through with this, you will come with me for that cruise in *The Night Moth.* Come! Promise!"

He flashed a smile at her.

"Go your own way! Pursue this bubble you call love! And when it bursts and your heart is broken you will come back to me to have it mended.

"That is the price I put upon my mercy. I ask no pledge. It shall be a debt of honour. We count that higher than a pledge."

Juliet suppressed a sudden tremor.

He stood up, gallantly raising her as he did so.

"And now we will go and look for your friends. Is all well, *ma chère?* You look pale."

She forced herself to smile.

"You are a preposterous person, Charles Rex. Yes, let us go!"

She turned with him towards the panelling, but she did not see by what trick he opened again the door by which they had entered.

She only saw, with a wild leap of the heart, Dick Green, upright, virile, standing against the dark hangings of the passage beyond.

He was breathing hard, as if he had been hurrying. He spoke to her exclusively, ignoring the man at her side.

"Will you come at once? Mrs. Fielding has been taken ill."

She started forward.

"Dick! Where is she?"

"Downstairs." Briefly he answered her. "She collapsed in one of the tents. They brought her into the house. She is in the Library."

*   *   *

Mr. Fielding met her, taking her urgently by the shoulder.

"Thank heaven, you're here at last!"

Looking at him, she saw him as a man suddenly stricken with age. His face was grey. He led her to a settee by the high oak fireplace, and there, white, inanimate as a waxen figure, she found Vera Fielding.

Fear pierced her, sharp as the thrust of a knife. She freed herself from Fielding's grip and knelt beside the silent form.

"Help me to lift her!" she commanded.

They raised her between them with infinite care. Then Lord Saltash, his queer face full of the most earnest concern, began to chafe one of the nerveless hands.

The Squire tramped ceaselessly up and down the room, his head on his chest. Every time he drew near his wife he glanced at her and swung away again, as one without hope.

After a brief interval the door opened to admit a silent-footed Butler bearing a tray. Lord Saltash turned upon him swiftly.

"Brandy, Billings? That's right. Find Mrs. Parsons! Tell her a lady has been taken ill in the Library. She had better get a bed ready, and have some boiling water handy." He looked at Juliet. "Anything else?"

She shook her head.

"No, nothing till the Doctor comes. I hope he won't be long."

There followed what seemed an interminable space of waiting, during which no change of any sort was apparent in the silent figure on the settee.

Then, after an eternity of suspense, the sombre-faced Butler opened the door again and ushered in the Doctor. Lord Saltash went to meet him and brought him to the settee. The Squire got up and came forward.

Dick stood for a moment, then turned and went back

to the Conservatory, where a few seconds later Lord Saltash joined him.

It seemed as if hours had passed before Juliet came out to join them.

Her face had an exhausted look, but she smiled faintly at the two men as she joined them.

"She is still living," she said. "The Doctor gives just a shade of hope. But . . ." She looked at Saltash. "He absolutely forbids her being moved . . . at all. I hope it won't be a terrible inconvenience to you."

"It will be a privilege to serve you—or your friends—in any way," Lord Saltash replied.

"You are very kind," she responded, and turned with a hint of embarrassment to Dick. "Mr. Fielding says that you will want to be getting back and there is no need to wait. Will you take the little car back to the Court?"

He looked back at her, standing very straight.

"In that case—I will go. Good-bye."

She held out her hand to him.

"I shall see you again," she said, and there was almost a touch of pleading in her voice.

His fingers closed and held.

"Yes," he replied, and smiled into her eyes with the words; a smile in which determination and tenderness strangely mingled. "You will certainly see me again."

And with that he was gone, striding between the massed flowers without looking back.

Chapter
Six

That Saturday-night concert at High Shale entailed a greater effort on Dick's part than any that had preceded it.

He forced himself to make it a success, but when it was over he was conscious of an overwhelming weariness that weighed him down like a physical burden.

He said good-night to the men, and prepared to depart, with a feeling that he was nearing the end of his endurance.

It was not soothing to nerves already on edge to be waylaid by Ashcott and made the unwilling recipient of gloomy forebodings.

"We shan't hold the men much longer," the manager said. "They're getting badly out-of-hand. There's talk of sending a deputation to Lord Wilchester or—failing him —Ivor Yardley, the Barrister chap who is in with him in this show."

"Yardley!" Dick uttered the name sharply.

"Yes, ever met him? He took over a directorship when he got engaged to Lord Wilchester's sister—Lady Joanna Farringmore. They're rather pinning their hopes on him, it seems. Do you know him at all?"

"I've met him—once," Dick replied. "Went to him for advice on a matter of business."

"Any good?" asked Ashcott.

"Oh yes, shrewd enough. Hardest-headed man at the Bar, I believe. I didn't know he was a director of this show. They won't get much out of him."

"Well, they're simmering," Ashcott said, as he prepared to depart. "They'll boil over before long. If they don't find a responsible representative they'll probably run amok and get up to mischief."

"Oh, man, stop croaking!" Dick said with weary irritation, and went away down the hill.

The sea lay leaden far below him, barely visible in the dimness.

Heavily he tramped over the ground where Juliet had lingered on that night of magic in the spring, and as he went he told himself that he had lost her.

Whatever the outcome of today's happenings, she would never be the same to him again. She had passed out of his reach. Her own world had claimed her again and there could be no return.

He recalled the regret in her eyes at parting. Surely—most surely—she had known that that was the end.

For her, the midsummer madness was over, burnt away like the glory of the gorse bushes about him. With a conviction that was beyond all reason he knew that they had come to a parting of the ways.

Again he felt the clinging of her arms as he had felt it only that afternoon. Again, against his lips there rose her quivering whisper:

"Just for today, Dick! Just for today!"

Yes, she had known even then. Even then for her the glory had begun to fade.

He clenched his hands in sudden fierce rebellion. It was unbearable. He would not endure it. This stroke of destiny, he would fight it with all the strength of his manhood.

He would overthrow this nameless barrier that had arisen between them. He would sacrifice all—all he had—to reach her. Somehow, whatever the struggle might cost, he would clasp her again, would hold her, against all the world.

The sea moaned with a dreary sound along the shore. A few heavy drops of rain fell round him. He came at length down the steep cliff path to the gate that led to the village.

And here to his surprise a shuffling footstep told him of the presence of another human being out in the desolate darkness. Dimly he discerned a bulky shape leaning against the rail.

He came up to it.

"Robin!" he said sharply.

A low voice answered him in startled accents:

"Oh, Dicky! I thought you were never coming!"

"What are you doing here?" Dick asked.

He took the boy by the shoulder with the words, and Robin cowered away.

"Come, old chap!" Dick said. "Get a hold on yourself! What's it all about?"

Robin's shoulders heaved convulsively; his hold tightened. He murmured some inarticulate words.

Dick bent over him.

"You haven't been up to mischief, have you? Robin, have you?" A sudden misgiving assailed him. "You haven't hurt anybody? Not Jack, for instance?"

"No," Robin answered.

But he added, a moment later, with a concentrated passion that sounded inexpressibly vindictive:

"I hate him! I do hate him! I wish he was dead!"

"What has Jack been doing or saying? Tell me! I've got to know."

Robin stirred uneasily.

"Don't want to tell you, Dicky."

Dick's hand pressed a little upon him.

"You must tell me," he urged. "When did you meet him?"

Robin hesitated in obvious reluctance.

"It was after supper," he said. "My head ached, and I went outside and he came down the drive. And he—and he laughed at me."

With difficulty he struggled on:

"Said that only a fool like me could help knowing that—you hadn't—a chance with any woman—so long as—so long as . . ."

He choked again and sank into quivering silence.

Dick's hand found the rough head and patted it very tenderly.

"But you're not fool enough to take what Jack says seriously, are you? You know as well as I do that there isn't a word of truth in it. Anyhow—the woman I love—isn't—that sort of woman."

Robin shifted his position uneasily. There was that in the words that vaguely stirred him. Dick had never spoken in that strain before.

Slowly, with a certain caution, he lifted his tear-stained face and peered up at his brother.

"You do want to marry Miss Moore then, Dicky?" he asked diffidently.

Dick looked straight back at him.

"Yes, I want her all right, Robin, but there are some pretty big obstacles in the way. I may get over them, and I may not. Time will prove."

His lips closed upon the words, and became again a single hard line. His look went beyond Robin and grew fixed. The boy watched him dumbly with awed curiosity.

Suddenly Dick moved, gripped him by the shoulders and pulled him upwards.

"There! Go to bed! And don't take any notice of what Jack says for the future!"

Robin blundered up obediently. Again there looked forth from his eyes the dog-like worship which he kept for Dick alone.

"I'll do—whatever you say, Dicky," he said very earnestly. "I—I'd die for you—I would!"

He spoke with immense effort, and all his heart was in the words.

Dick smiled quizzically.

"Instead of which, I only want you to show a little ordinary common or garden sense. Think you can do that for me?"

"I'll try, Dicky," he answered humbly.

"Yes, all right. You try!" Dick said, and got up, more moved than he cared to show.

He turned to go, but paused to say:

"And don't forget I'm rather fond of you, my boy!" And, with a brief smile over his shoulder, he went away.

No, Robin was not likely to forget that, seeing that Dick's love for him was his safeguard from all evil, and his love for Dick was the mainspring of his life.

Dick's words "the woman I love" had sunk deep, deep into his soul. And he knew with that intuition which cannot err that his love for Juliet was the greatest thing life held for him, or ever could hold again.

And the driving force gripped Robin's soul afresh as he lay wide-eyed in the smothering gloom of the night. Whatever happened, whoever suffered, Dicky must have his heart's desire.

* * *

For five days Juliet scarcely left Vera Fielding's side. During those five days Vera lay at the point of death, and though her husband was constantly with her, it was to Juliet that she clung through all the terrible phases of weakness, breathlessness, and pain.

Juliet seldom left Vera's bedside in the afternoon, for it was then, in the heat of the day, that she usually suffered most. But today she had been better.

Today for the first time she was able to turn her head and smile and even to murmur a few sentences without distress. Her eyes dwelt with a wistful affection upon Juliet's quiet face.

"Quite comfortable?" Juliet asked her gently.

"Quite," Vera whispered. "But you . . . you look so tired."

Juliet smiled at her.

"I daresay I shall fall asleep if you do."

"You ought to have a long rest," said Vera, and then her heavy eyes brightened and went beyond her as her husband's tall figure came softly in from the Conservatory.

He came to her side, stooped over her, and took her hand. Her fingers closed weakly about his.

"Send her to bed!" she whispered. "She is tired. You come instead!"

He bent and kissed her forehead with a tenderness that made her cling more closely.

"Will you go to bed, Juliet," he said in that new gentle voice of his, "and leave me in charge?"

Juliet found herself yielding without misgiving, though till then he had been allowed at Vera's bedside only for a few minutes at a time.

She paused to give him one or two directions regarding medicine, then went quietly to the door of the Conservatory.

Columbus sprang to greet her with a joy that convulsed him from head to tail, and she gathered him up in her arms and took him with her.

In the Great Hall outside she found Lord Saltash loitering. He came at once to meet her, and had taken Columbus from her before she realised his intention.

"He is too heavy for you, *ma chère*," he said with his quizzing smile. "Lend him to me for the afternoon! He's getting disgracefully fat. I'll take him for a walk."

Relieved of Columbus's weight, she became suddenly and overpoweringly aware of a dwindling of her strength.

She said no word, but her face must have betrayed her, for the next thing she knew, Lord Saltash's arm was like a coiled spring about her, impelling her towards the grand staircase.

"I'll take you to your room, *Juliette*," he said. "You might miss the way by yourself. You're awfully tired, aren't you?"

It was absurd, but a curious desire to weep possessed her.

"Yes, I know," replied Lord Saltash, with his semi-comic tenderness. "Don't mind me! I knew you'd come to it sooner or later. You're not used to playing the sister of mercy, are you, *ma mie*, though it becomes you—vastly well."

He guided her up the branching staircase to the gallery above, bringing her finally to a tall oak door at the farther end.

"Here is your chamber of sleep, *Juliette*," he said lightly. "I leave you to your dreams."

He went away along the gallery, and she entered the room and shut herself in.

For a second or two she stood quite motionless in the great luxurious apartment. Then slowly she went forward to the wide-flung window, and stood there, gazing blankly forth over the distant fir-clad Park.

He had said that he would see her again. It seemed so long ago. And all through this difficult time of strain and anxiety he had done nothing . . . nothing.

Ah, well! Perhaps it was better to end it all like this, that midsummer madness of theirs that had already endured too long! They had lived such widely sundered lives. How could they ever have hoped ultimately to bridge the gulf between?

Perhaps Dick himself had foreseen it long since, down on that golden shore when first he had sought to dissuade her from going to the Court!

Her heart contracted at the memory. How sweet those early days had been! But the roses had faded, the nightingales had ceased to sing. It was all over now, all over. The dream was shattered, and she felt as though all life had been drained from her.

* * *

From the day that Juliet relinquished her perpetual vigil, the improvement in Vera Fielding was almost uninterrupted.

She recovered her strength very slowly, but her progress was marked by a happy certainty that none who saw her could question. She still leant upon Juliet, but it was her husband alone who could call that deep contentment into her eyes.

The nearness of death had done for them what no circumstances of life had ever accomplished.

All Vera's arrogance had vanished in her husband's presence, just as his curt imperiousness had given place to the winning dominance which he knew so well how to wield.

"I wonder if we shall go on like this when I'm well again," she said to him on an evening of rose-coloured dusk in early August, when he was sitting by her side.

"Like what?" asked Edward Fielding.

She smiled at him from her pillow.

"Well, spoiling each other in this way. Will you never be overbearing and dictatorial? Shall I never be furious and hateful to you again?"

"God bless you, my dear!" he said. "You needn't be afraid. I've learnt my lesson, and I shan't forget it."

"The lesson of love!" she murmured, holding his hand against her heart.

"Yes. Juliet began the teaching. A wonderful girl, that. She seems to know everything."

"She is wonderful," Vera agreed thoughtfully. "I sometimes think she has had a hard life. She says so little about herself."

"She has moved among a fairly rapid lot," observed the Squire. "Lord Saltash is intimate enough to call her by her Christian name."

"Does he ever talk about her?" asked Vera, interested, in spite of her weakness.

"Not much," replied the Squire.

"You think he is fond of her at all?"

"I don't know. He doesn't see much of her. I haven't quite got his measure yet. He isn't the sort of man I thought he was, anyway."

"Then it wasn't true about Lady Joanna Farringmore?" questioned Vera.

"Oh, that!"

He stood, hesitating. But there were certainly footsteps in the Conservatory.

"I'll tell you some other time, my dear," he said gently. "Here comes Juliet to turn me out!"

He turned as she entered and greeted her with a smile. Vera was still clinging to his hand.

Juliet slowly came forward. Her face was pale. She was holding a letter in her hand. She looked from one to the other for a second or two in silence.

The Squire was looking at her attentively.

"What is the matter?" he asked suddenly.

She met his look steadily, though he felt it to be with an effort. Then quietly she turned to Vera.

"I have just had a letter," she said, "from a friend who is in trouble. Do you think you can spare me . . . for a little while?"

Vera stretched a hand towards her.

"You will come back to me?" she asked.

"I will certainly come back," Juliet answered, "even if I can't stay. But now that you are able to sit up, you will need me less. You will take care of her, Mr. Fielding?"

He nodded.

"You may be sure of that—the utmost care. When must you go?"

He was looking at her closely, his eyes deeply searching.

Juliet hesitated.

"Do you think . . . tonight?"

"Certainly. Then you will want a car. Have you told Lord Saltash?" He turned to the door.

"No, I have only just heard. I believe he has gone to town." Juliet gently laid down the hand she was holding.

"I will come back," she said again, and followed him.

He drew the door closed behind him. They faced each other in the dimness of the Hall. The Squire's mouth was twitching uncontrollably.

"Now, Juliet!" His voice had a ring of sternness; he put his hand on her shoulder, gripping unconsciously. "For heaven's sake, out with it! It isn't Dick?"

"No . . . Robin!"

"Ah!" He drew a deep breath and straightened himself, his other hand over his eyes. Then in a moment he was looking at her again. His grip relaxed. "Forgive me! Did I hurt you?"

She gave him a faint smile.

"It doesn't matter. You understand, don't you? I must go to Dick."

He nodded.

"Yes—yes! Is the boy dead?"

"No. It was a fall over the cliff. It happened last night. They didn't find him for hours. He is going fast. Jack brought me this." She glanced down at the letter in her hand.

He made a half-gesture to take it, then checked himself sharply.

"I beg your pardon, Juliet, I hardly know what I'm doing. It's from Dick, is it?"

Very quietly she gave it to him.

"You may read it. You have a right to know."

He gave her an odd look.

"May I? Are you sure?"

"Read it!"

He opened it. His fingers were trembling. She stood at his shoulder and read it with him. The words were few, containing the bald statement, but no summons.

The Squire read them, breathing heavily. Suddenly he thrust his arm round Juliet and held her fast.

"Juliet! You'll be good to my boy—good to Dick?"

Her eyes met his.

"That is why I am going to him." She took the note, and folded it, standing within the circle of his arm.

"I'd go to him myself if I could," the Squire went on unevenly. "He'll feel this damnably. He was simply devoted to that unfortunate boy."

"I know," replied Juliet.

Again he put his hand to his eyes.

"I've been a beast about Robin. Ask him to forgive me, Juliet! Make him understand!"

"He will understand," Juliet said quietly.

He looked at her again.

"Don't let him fret, Juliet! You'll comfort him, won't you? You love him, don't you?"

"Yes," she answered.

"God bless you for that! I can't tell you what he is to me—can't explain."

"I understand."

"What?" He stared at her for a moment. "What—do you understand?"

"I know what he is to you," she said gently. "I have known for a long time. Never mind how! Nobody told me. It just came to me one day."

"Ah!" Impulsively he broke in. "You see everything. I'm afraid of you, Juliet. But look here! You won't—you won't make him suffer for my sins?"

Her hand pressed his arm.

"What am I?" she said. "Have I any right to judge anyone? Besides, do you think I could possibly go to him if I did not feel that nothing on earth matters now . . . except our love!"

She spoke with deep emotion. She was quivering from head to foot. He bent very low to kiss the hand upon his arm.

"And you will have your reward," he said huskily. "Don't forget—it's the only thing in life that really counts! There's nothing else—nothing else."

Juliet stood quite still, looking down at the bent grey head.

"I wonder," she said slowly. "I wonder . . . if Dick . . . in his heart . . . thinks the same!"

*　　*　　*

The August dusk had deepened into night when the open car from the Court pulled up at the schoolhouse gate.

"Do you mind going in alone?" whispered Jack. "I'll wait inside the Park gates to take you back."

"You needn't wait," Juliet replied. "I shall spend the night at the Court . . . unless I am wanted here."

She descended with the words. She had never liked Jack Green, and she was thankful that the rapid journey was over.

In the dark little porch she hesitated. The silence was intense. Then, as she stood in uncertainty, from across the bare playground there came a call.

"Juliet!"

She turned swiftly. He was standing in the dark doorway of the school, the vague light of the rising moon gleaming deathly on his face. He did not move to meet her.

She went to him, reached out hands to him that he did not take, and clasped him by the shoulders.

"Oh, you poor boy!" she said.

His arms held her close for a moment or two, then they relaxed.

"I don't know why I sent for you."

"You didn't send for me, Dick," she answered gently. "But I think you wanted me all the same."

He groaned.

"Wanted you! I've craved for you. You told the Squire?"

"Yes. He said . . ."

He broke in upon her with fierce bitterness:

"He was pleased, of course! I knew he would be. That's why I couldn't send the message to him. It had to be you."

"Dick! Dick! He wasn't pleased! You don't know what you're saying. He was most terribly sorry." She put her arm through his with a very tender gesture. "Won't you take me inside and tell me all about it?"

He gave a hard shudder.

"I don't know if I can, Juliet. It's been so awful."

"Oh, my dear!"

He put his hands over his face.

"Juliet, it was hell!"

Again a convulsive shudder caught him. Juliet's arm went round him. She held his head against her breast.

"It's over now," she whispered. "Thank God for that!"

He leant upon her for a space.

"Yes, it's over. At least he died in peace," he said, and drew a hard, quivering breath.

Then he stood up again.

"Juliet, I'm so sorry. Come inside!" He turned and pushed open the door. "Wait a minute while I light up!"

She did not wait but followed him closely, and stood beside him while he lighted a lamp on the wall. He turned from doing so and smiled at her, and she saw that though his face was ghastly, he was his own master again.

"How did you get here?" he asked. "Who took the note? The Doctor promised to get it delivered."

"Jack brought it. I came back with him."

"Jack!"

His brows drew together suddenly. She saw his black eyes gleam. For a moment he said nothing further.

"If Jack comes anywhere near me tonight, I shall kill him!" he said very quietly.

"Dick!" she said in amazement.

There was a certain awful intentness in his look.

"I hold him responsible for this. I know what I am saying. He is directly responsible."

His voice faltered.

"My boy died for my sake, because he believed what Jack told him—that no woman would ever consent to marry me while he lived."

"Oh, Dick! You don't mean . . . he did it . . . on purpose!" Juliet's voice was quick with pain. "Dick . . . surely . . . surely . . . it wasn't that! You are making a mistake!"

"No. It is no mistake," he replied with sombre conviction. "I know it. It's been preying on his mind ever since. He hasn't been well. He . . ."

He stopped himself.

"There's no need to distress you over this. Is he—is Jack waiting to take you back?"

"No," Juliet replied quietly.

His brows went up.

"You are sleeping at the Court? I'll take you there."

"I'm not going yet, Dick," she said gently, "unless you turn me out."

His face quivered unexpectedly. He turned from her.

"There's nothing to wait for."

But Juliet stood motionless. Her eyes went down the long bare room with its empty forms and ink-splashed desks. She thought it the most desolate place she had ever seen.

After an interval of blank silence Dick spoke again.

"Don't you stay! I'm not myself tonight. I can't think. It was awfully good of you to come. But don't stay!"

"Dick!" she said.

At the sound of her voice he turned. His eyes looked at her out of such a depth of misery as pierced her to the heart. She saw his hands clench against his sides.

"Oh, my God!" he said under his breath.

"Dick!" she said again very earnestly. "Don't send me away! Let me help you!"

"You can't. You've been too good to me already."

"You wouldn't say that to me if I were your wife."

He flinched sharply.

"Juliet! Don't torture me! I've had as much as I can stand tonight."

She held out her hands to him with a gesture superbly simple.

"My darling, I will marry you tomorrow if you will have me."

He stood for a long second staring at her. Then she saw his face change and harden. The ascetic look that she had noticed long ago came over it like a mask.

"No!" he said. "No!"

Again he turned from her.

"Can you imagine how Cain felt when he said that his punishment was greater than he could bear? That's how I feel tonight. I am like Cain. Whatever I touch is cursed."

"You are not like Cain," she said gently. "And even if you were, do you think I should love you any the less?"

He made a desperate gesture.

"Would you love me if I were a murderer?"

"I love you . . . whatever you are."

He turned upon her almost like an animal at bay.

"I am a murderer, Juliet!" he said, a terrible fire in his eyes.

In spite of herself she flinched, so awful was his look.

"Dick, what do you mean?"

He flung out a hand as if to keep her from him, though she had not moved.

"I will tell you what I mean, and then you will go. On the night Robin was born—I killed his father!"

"Dick!"

He went on rapidly:

"I was a boy at the time. My mother was dying. They sent me to fetch him. He was at The Three Tuns—drinking! I hung about till he came out. He was blind drunk, and the night was dark. He took the wrong path that led to the cliff, and I let him go."

His voice sounded hopeless.

"In the morning they found him on the rocks—dead."

He stood stiffly facing her.

"I never repented. But I suppose God doesn't allow these things. Anyway, I've been punished—pretty heavily. I got fond of the boy. He was the only thing left to care for. He took the place of everything else. And now because of a damnable lie . . ."

Something seemed to rise in his throat; he paused, struggling with himself; finally he went on jerkily, with difficulty:

"One more thing—you'd better know. It'll help you to forget me. The man I killed was not my own father—except in name. My mother refused to marry the man she loved because his people threatened to disown him. She gave herself instead to the scoundrel whose name I bear—just to set him free."

Again he stopped. Juliet had moved and her eyes were shining with a light that made her beautiful. She reached him and stood before him.

"Dick," she said. "I am not like your mother. I've been fighting against it, but it's too strong for me. I have got to marry the man I love."

He made an impotent gesture, and she saw that he was trembling.

She stood a moment, then reached out, took his arms, and drew them gently round her.

"Are you still trying to send me away? Because ... it's stronger than both of us, Dick, and I'm not going ... I'm not going!"

He looked into the shining, steadfast eyes, and suddenly the desperate strain was over. His resistance snapped.

"God forgive me!" he said under his breath, and caught her passionately close.

As he clasped her she felt the wild throbbing of his heart. He kissed her, and in his kiss there was more than the lover's adoration. It held the demand and mastery of matehood. By it he claimed and sealed her for his own.

When his hold relaxed, she made no effort to withdraw herself. She leant against him, gasping a little, but her eyes, with the glory yet shining in them, were still raised to his.

"So that's settled, is it?" She spoke with a quivering smile. "You are quite sure, Dick?"

His hands were clasped behind her. His look had a certain burning quality, as if he challenged all the world for her possession.

"What am I to say to you, Juliet?" His voice was low and deeply vibrant. "I can't deny my other self—can I?"

"I don't know. You were very near it, weren't you? I thought you had ... all these weeks."

"Ah!" His brows contracted. "Will you forgive me, Juliet? I've had an infernal time."

And then suddenly he took her face between his hands, looking closely into her eyes.

"Don't you care about all the horrible things I've told you?" he asked. "Does it make no difference at all to you?"

She was still smiling, a tremulous smile.

"It doesn't seem much like it, does it? I'm not such a saint myself, Dick. And I couldn't help knowing ages ago ... what made the Squire so fond of you."

"Juliet!" He gazed at her. "How on earth did you find out?"

She coloured deeply under his look.

"You are rather alike ... in some ways. It was partly

that and partly being . . . well, rather interested in you, I suppose. And Mrs. Rickett told me as much of your family history as she knew before I ever met you. So, you see, I didn't have much to fill in."

"And still it makes no difference?"

She shook her head.

"None whatever. I'm just glad for your sake that the man you hated so was not your father. But I think you go rather far, Dick, when you say you killed him."

The hard, onyx-like glitter shone again in his eyes.

"No, it was not an exaggeration. I was a murderer that night. I meant him to go to his death. When he was dead I was glad. He had tortured the only being I loved on earth.

"I believed he was my father for quite a long time after—till the Squire came home, and I told him the whole story."

He smiled rather bitterly.

"Then—in an impulsive moment—he told me the truth. He cared about my mother's death—cared badly. They would have been married by that time if her husband hadn't turned up again. It was two lives spoilt."

He drew her to him again. The desperate misery had passed from his face, but he looked worn out.

"What on earth should I do without you?"

"I don't know, darling," she answered tenderly. "I hope you are not going to try any longer, are you?"

His lips were near her own.

"Juliet, will you stay within reach till after the funeral?"

"Yes," she breathed.

"And then—then—will you marry me?"

His whisper was even lower than hers. The man's whole being pulsed in the words.

Her arms went round his neck.

"I will, dearest."

His breath came quickly.

"And if—if—later you come upon some things that hurt you—things you don't understand—will you remember how I've been handicapped and—forgive me?"

Her eyes looked straight up to his. They held a shadowy smile.

"Dick . . . I was just going . . . to say that . . . to you!"

He pressed her to his heart.

"Ah, my Juliet! Could anything matter to us—anything on earth—except our love?"

In the deep silence her lips answered his. There was no further need for words.

Chapter
Seven

"I'm not quite sure that I call this fair play," said Lord Saltash with a comical twist of the eyebrows. "I didn't expect all these developments in so short a time."

"There are no further rules to this game," replied Juliet. "Whoever wins ... or loses ... no-one has any right to complain."

He made a face at her.

"That's your point of view. And what am I to say when I meet Muff and all the rest of the clan again and tell them you are married?"

She gave a slight shrug.

"Do you think it matters? They are much too busy chasing after their own affairs to give me a second thought."

He leant back in his chair, his hands behind his head, and contemplated her with a criticism that lasted several seconds. His dark face wore its funny, monkeyish look of regret, half-wistful and half-feigned.

"I wish ..." he said suddenly. "I wish I'd come down here when you first began to rusticate."

"Why?" asked Juliet, with her level eyes upon him.

He laughed and sprang abruptly to his feet.

"¿Quién sabe? I might have turned rustic too—pious also, my *Juliette!* Think of it! Life isn't fair to me. Why am I condemned always to ride the desert alone?"

"Mainly because you ride too hard," replied Juliet. "None but you can keep up the pace. Ah!"

115

She turned her head quickly, and the swift colour flooded her face.

"Ah!" mocked Lord Saltash softly, watching her. "Is it Romeo's step that I hear?"

Columbus wagged his tail in welcome as Dick Green came round the corner of the Ricketts' cottage and walked down under the apple trees to join them.

He greeted Saltash with the quiet self-assurance of a man who treads his own ground. There was no hint of hostility in his bearing.

"I've been expecting you," he said coolly.

"Have you?" said Lord Saltash, a gleam of malicious humour in his eyes. "I thought there was something of the conquering hero about you. I have come—naturally—to congratulate you on your marriage."

"Thank you," replied Dick, and seated himself on the bench beside Juliet and Columbus. "That is very magnanimous."

"It is," agreed Lord Saltash. "But if I had known what was in the wind while I was away, I might have carried it still further and offered you Burchester Castle for the honeymoon."

"How kind of you!" Juliet said. "But we prefer cottages to Castles, don't we, Dick?"

She laughed a little.

"It doesn't much matter where you are so long as you are happy. At the same time, Dick is within reach of the miners, who are being rather tiresome."

"Oh, those infernal miners!" said Saltash, and looked at Dick. "How long do you think you are going to keep them in hand?"

"I can't say," answered Dick somewhat briefly. "I don't advise Lord Wilchester or Ivor Yardley to come down here till something has been done to settle them."

A sudden silence fell.

"So you know Yardley, do you?" Lord Saltash spoke softly. "Rather a brute in some ways, cold-blooded as a fish and wily as a serpent, but interesting—distinctly interesting. When did you meet him?"

"Early this year. I consulted him on a matter of business. I have no private acquaintance with him."

Dick was looking straight at Lord Saltash with a certain contempt in his face.

"You evidently are on terms of intimacy with him."

"Oh, quite!" said Lord Saltash readily. "He knows me—almost as well as you do. And I know him—even better."

He smiled wickedly.

"I was saying to *Juliette* just now that I believe he shares the general impression that I have got Lady Jo Farringmore somewhere up my sleeve.

"She did the rabbit-trick, you know, a week or two before the wedding, and because I was to have been best man I somehow got the blame."

Juliet came out of her silence.

"Dick has rather strong opinions on the subject, Charles, so please don't be flippant about it!"

Lord Saltash looked at her, then he sprang up in his abrupt fashion.

"I'm going. Thanks for putting up with me for so long. I had to come and see you, *Juliette*. You are one of the very few capable of appreciating me at my full value."

"I hope you will come again," she replied.

He bowed low over her hand.

"If I can ever serve you in any way, I hope you will give me the privilege. Farewell, most estimable Romeo! You may yet live to greet me as a friend."

He was gone with the words, leaving behind him an intense silence.

Then Juliet, very quiet of mien and level of brow, got up and went to Dick, who had risen at the departure of the visitor. She put her hand through his arm and held it closely.

"You are not to be unkind to my friends, Richard. It is the one thing I can't allow."

He looked at her with some sternness, but his free hand closed at once upon hers.

"I hate to think of you on terms of intimacy with that bounder."

She laid her cheek with a very loving gesture against his shoulder.

"Ah, don't throw stones!" she pleaded gently. "There are so few of us without sin."

His arm was about her in a moment, all his hardness vanished.

"My own girl!"

She held his hand in both her own.

"Do you know . . . sometimes . . . I lie awake at night and wonder . . . and wonder . . . whatever you would have thought of me . . . if you had known me in the old days."

"Is that it?" he said very tenderly. "And you thought I was sleeping like a log and didn't know."

She laughed rather tremulously, her face turned from him.

"It isn't always possible to bury the past, is it, however hard we try? I hope you'll make allowances for that, Dick, if ever I shock your sense of propriety."

"I shall make allowances, because you are the one and only woman I worship—or have ever worshipped— and I can't see you in any other light."

"How dear of you, Dicky!" she murmured. "And how rash!"

"Am I such an unutterable prig? I feel myself that I have got extra-fastidious since knowing you."

She laughed at that.

"You're not a prig, darling. You are just an honourable and upright gentleman. What have you been doing all this time? I should have come to look for you if Saltash hadn't turned up."

Dick's brows were slightly drawn.

"I've been talking to Jack."

"Jack!" She opened her eyes. "Dick! I hope you haven't been quarrelling!"

He smiled at her anxious face, though somewhat grimly.

"My dear, I don't quarrel with people like Jack. I took the opportunity for a straight talk, with the result that he leaves tomorrow—for good."

Dick's lips came together in a hard, compelling line.

"Are you never going to forgive him?" asked Juliet.

His eyes had a stony glitter.

"It's hardly a matter for forgiveness. When anyone has done you an irreparable injury, the only thing left is to try and forget it and the person responsible for it as quickly as possible. I simply want to be rid of him, and to wipe out all memory of him."

"Do you always want to do that with the people who injure you?"

He looked at her, caught by something in her tone.

"Yes, I think so. Why?"

"Oh, never mind why!" she said, with a faint laugh that sounded oddly passionate. "I just want to find out what sort of man you are, that's all."

She would have turned away from him with the words, but he held her with a certain dominance.

"No, Juliet! Wait! Tell me—isn't it reasonable to want to get free of anyone who wrongs you—to shake him off, kick him off if necessary—anyway, to have done with him?"

"I haven't said it was unreasonable," she answered, but she was trembling as she spoke and her face was averted.

"Look at me!" he said. "What? Am I such a monster as all that? Juliet—my dear, don't be silly! What are you afraid of? Surely not of me!"

She turned her face to him with a quivering smile.

"No! Dick! But to be quite honest, I am rather afraid of the hard side of you. It is so very uncompromising. If I ever come up against it . . . I believe I shall run away!"

"Not you!" he answered, trying to look into the soft, downcast eyes "What I have—I hold!"

She resisted him for a second or two, holding him from her, half-mocking, half in earnest. Then, as his hold tightened, encompassing her, she submitted with a low laugh.

But when at last his hold relaxed, she took his hand and pressed a deep kiss into his palm.

"That is . . . a free gift, Dicky. And it is worth more than all the having and holding in the world."

* * *

It was on a misty evening of autumn that Vera Fielding entered her husband's house once more like a bride returning from her wedding-trip.

"I fell as if we have been away for years and years," she said to him as they stood together before the blazing fire in the Drawing-Room. "Isn't it strange, Edward? Only three months in reality, and such a difference!"

He smiled upon her indulgently. They had grown very near to each other during their cruise. To him also their homecoming held something of bridal gladness. The love that shone in her eyes whenever they met his own stirred him to the depths.

He had never deemed her capable of such affection in the old days. It had changed his whole world.

"Do you remember that awful day when we quarrelled about Dick Green?" said Vera suddenly.

He held her hand in his.

"Don't! Don't remind me of it!"

She put up a hand and stroked his iron-grey hair.

"Well, we shan't quarrel about young Green any more," she said.

"I wonder," the Squire answered, not looking at her.

"I don't." She spoke with confidence. "I'm going to be tremendously nice to him ... not for Juliet's sake ... for yours."

"Thank you, my dear," he said, with an odd humility of utterance that came strangely from him. "I shall appreciate your kindness. As you know, I am very fond of Dick."

"You were going to tell me why once."

He took her hand and held it for a moment.

"I will tell you tonight."

The maid came in then with the tea-tray and they had no further intimate talk.

The Squire became restless and walked about the room while he drank his tea. When he had finished, he went away, and Vera was left to dress.

Her maid was still putting the final touches when there came a low knock at the door. She turned sharply from her mirror.

"Is that you, Juliet? Come in! Come in!"

Quietly the door opened and Juliet entered.

"My dear!" said Vera, and met her impulsively in the middle of the room.

"I had to come up," Juliet said. "I hope you don't mind, but neither Dick nor I can manage to feel like ordinary guests in this house."

She was smiling as she spoke. The white scarf was thrown back from her hair. The gracious womanliness of her struck Vera afresh with its charm.

She held her and looked at her.

"My dear Juliet, it does me good to see you. How is Dick? And how is Columbus?"

"They are both downstairs, and one is working too hard and the other not hard enough."

"Then suppose we go downstairs?" Vera said.

They went down to find Dick and Columbus patiently waiting in the Hall.

Vera gave Dick a warmer welcome than she had ever extended to him before, and found in the instant response of his smile some reason for wonder at her previous dislike.

Perhaps contact with Juliet had helped to banish the satire to which in the old days she had so strongly objected.

When the Squire came down they were all chatting amicably round the fire, and he smiled swift approval upon his wife before he turned to greet his guests.

"Hullo, Dick!" he said, as their hands met. "Still running the same old show?"

"For the present, Sir."

They had not met since the occasion of Dick and Juliet's marriage, when the Squire had come over to give her away.

He had been very kind to them both during the brief hour that he had spent with them, and the memory of it still lingered warmly in Juliet's heart. She had grown very fond of the Squire.

There were no awkward moments during that dinner, which was more like a family gathering than Juliet had thought possible.

Dick was apparently in good spirits that night, and he was plainly at his ease. When they left the table Vera gave him a smiling invitation to come and play to them.

"I haven't brought the old banjo, but I'll make my wife sing. She is going to help me this winter at the club concerts."

"Brave Juliet!" said Vera, as she went out. "I wouldn't face that crowd of roughs for a King's ransom."

"She has nothing to be afraid of," answered Dick with quick confidence. "I wouldn't let her do it if there were any danger."

"They seem to be in an ugly mood just now," said the Squire.

"Yes, I know." Dick turned back to him, closing the door. "But, taken the right way, they are still manageable.

"There is just a chance that we may keep them in hand if that fellow Ivor Yardley can be induced to see reason. The rest of the Wilchester crew don't care a damn, but he has more brains. I'm counting on him."

"Perhaps we could get him down here," suggested the Squire.

Dick gave him a swift look.

"I've thought of that," he answered.

"Well?" said the Squire.

Dick hesitated for a moment.

"I'm not sure that I want him. He and Lord Saltash are friends, for one thing. And there are, besides, various reasons."

"You don't like Saltash?" asked the Squire.

Dick laughed a little.

"I don't hate him—though I feel as if I ought to. He's a queer fish. I don't trust him."

"You're jealous?"

Dick nodded.

"Very likely. He has an uncanny attraction for women. I wanted to kick him the last time we met."

"And what did Juliet say?"

"Oh, Juliet read me a lecture and told me I wasn't to. But I think the less we see of each other the better—if I am to keep on my best behaviour, that is."

"It's a good thing someone can manage you," remarked the Squire. "Juliet is a wonderful peacemaker. But even she couldn't keep you from coming to loggerheads with Jack, apparently. What was that fight about?"

Dick's brows contracted.

"It wasn't a fight, Sir," he said shortly. "I've never fought Jack in my life. He did an infernal thing and I made him quit, that's all."

"What did he do?" asked the Squire.

Then as Dick made a gesture of refusal, he went on:

"Damn it, man, he was in my employment, anyway!
I've a right to know why he cleared out."

Dick pushed back his chair abruptly and rose. He
turned his back on the Squire while he poked the blazing
logs with his foot.

"Yes, you've a perfect right to know," he said, speaking jerkily, his head bent. "He was responsible for my
boy's death. That's why I made him go."

Again for a space he stopped, then with a sudden
fierce impatience jerked on.

"You may remember saying to me once—no, a hundred times over—that I should never get anywhere so
long as I kept my boy with me—never find success—or
happiness—never marry—all that sort of rot."

He glanced upwards for a second with working
lips.

"I can't dress this up in polite language. Jack said to
my boy Robin what you had said to me. And he believed
it, and so—made an end."

He drew his breath hard between his teeth and
straightened himself, putting the Squire's arm gently from
him.

"Committed suicide!" ejaculated the Squire.

Dick's hands were clenched.

"Do you call it that, when a man lays down his life
for his friends?"

He turned away with the words as if he could endure
no more, and walked to the end of the room.

The Squire stood and watched him dumbly, more
moved than he cared to show. At length he spoke, his tone
an odd mixture of peremptoriness and persuasion.

"Dick!"

Dick jerked his head without turning or speaking.

"Are you blaming me for this?" the Squire asked.

Dick turned. His face was pale, his eyes fiercely
bright.

"You, Sir! Do you think I'd have sat at your table if I
did?"

"I don't know," the Squire replied sombrely. "You're
fond of telling me I have no claim on you, but I have, for
all that. There is a bond between us that you can't get
away from, however hard you try.

"You think I'm only pleased to know that you're free from your burden at last, eh, Dick, and that your trouble doesn't count with me? Think I've never had any of my own, perhaps?"

He spoke with a half-smile, but there was that in his voice that made Dick come swiftly back to him down the long room; nor did he pause when he reached him. His hand went out to the Squire's arm and gripped it hard.

"I'm awfully sorry, Sir. If you understand—you'll forgive me."

"I do understand, Dick. I know I've been hard on you about that poor boy. I'm infernally sorry for the whole wretched business. But—as you say—you'll get over it. You've got Juliet!"

"Yes, thank God! I don't know how I should endure life without her. She's all I have."

The Squire's face contracted a little.

"No-one else, Dick?"

Dick glanced up.

"And you, Sir," he amended with a smile. "I'm afraid I'm rather apt to take you for granted. I suppose that's the bond you've spoken of. I haven't—you know I haven't—the least desire to get away from it."

"Thank you," responded the Squire, stifling a sigh. "Life has been pretty damnable to us both, Dick. We might have been—we ought to have been—much more to each other."

"There's no tie more enduring than friendship," said Dick quickly. "You and I are friends—always will be."

He gave the Squire a straight and very friendly look, then wheeled round swiftly at the opening of the door.

They were standing side by side as Vera threw it impatiently wide. She stood a second on the threshold, staring at them.

"Are you never coming in? I thought . . . I thought . . . " she stammered suddenly and turned white.

Dick instantly went forward to her.

"Yes, Mrs. Fielding. We're coming now. Awfully sorry to have kept you waiting. Take my arm, I say! You look tired."

He offered and she accepted almost instinctively. Her

hand trembled on his arm as they left the room, and he suddenly and very impulsively laid his own upon it.

It was a protective impulse that moved him, but a moment later he adjusted the position by asking a favour of her, for the first time in the whole of their acquaintance.

"Mrs. Fielding, please, after today give me the privilege off numbering myself among your friends!"

She looked at him oddly, seeking to cover her agitation with a quivering assumption of her old arrogance. But something in his face deterred her.

It was not the man's way to solicit favours, and somehow, since he had humbled himself to ask, she had it not in her to refuse.

"Very well, Dick, I grant you that."

"Thank you," he answered, and gently released her hand.

It was the swiftest and one of the most complete victories of his life.

* * *

It was nearly two hours later that Vera, sitting alone before her fire, turned with a slight start at the sound of her husband's steps.

"Still up?" he said.

Again at his approach she made a more pronounced movement of shrinking.

"I've been waiting for you," she said rather hopelessly.

He came to her, stood looking down at her, the old bitter frown struggling with a more kindly expression on his face. He was obviously waiting for something with no pleasant sense of anticipation.

But Vera did not speak. She only sat drawn together, her fingers locked and her eyes downcast. She was using her utmost strength to keep herself in hand.

"Well?" he said at length, a faint ring of irritation in his voice. "Have you nothing to say to me now that I have come?"

Her lips quivered a little.

"I don't think there is anything to be said. I knew . . . I felt . . . it was too good to last."

"It's over then, is it?" he said, the bitterness gaining the upper hand because of the misery at his heart. "The indiscretions of my youth have placed me finally beyond the pale. Is that it?"

She gripped her hands together a little more tightly.

"I think you have been . . . you are . . . rather cruel. If only you had told me."

He made a gesture of exasperation.

"My dear girl, for heaven's sake, look at the thing fairly if you can! How long have I known you well enough to let you into my secrets? I meant to tell you—as you know. It wasn't cowardice that held me back. It was consideration for you."

She glanced at him momentarily.

"I see," she said in that small quivering voice of hers that told so little of the wild tumult within her.

"Well," he said harshly. "And that is my condemnation, is it? Henceforth I am to be thrust outside—a sinner beyond redemption. Is that it?"

"Oh, Edward, why did this have to happen? We were so happy before."

That pierced him, the utter desolation of her, the pain that was too deep for reproach. He bent to her, all the bitterness gone from his face.

"My dear," he said in a voice that shook, "can't you see how I loathe myself for hurting you like this?"

And then suddenly, so suddenly that neither knew exactly how it happened, they were linked together.

She was clinging to him with a rush of piteous tears, and he was kneeling beside her, holding her fast pressed against his heart, murmuring over her brokenly, passionately, such words of tenderness as she had never heard from him before.

She slipped her arm about his neck and pressed her cheek to his.

"Oh, Edward, darling, don't . . . don't keep anything from me ever again! If only I'd known sooner, things might have been so different. I feel as if I have never known you till now."

"Have you forgiven me?" he asked, his grey head bent.

She turned her lips again to him.

"My dear, of course ... of course. Will you tell me about her? Did she mean very much to you?"

His arm tightened about her.

"My darling, it's nearly twenty-three years ago that she died. Yes, I loved her."

He paused a moment, then as she was silent he went on more steadily:

"She was eighteen and I was twenty-two when it began. We loved each other like mad. It got beyond all reason—all restraint. We didn't look ahead, either of us."

He leant his head against her.

"We were found out at last, and there was a fearful row with my people. I wanted to take her away then and there, and marry her. But she wouldn't hear of it—neither would her aunt—a hard, proud woman.

"I didn't know then, no-one knew, that she was expecting a child, or I'd have defied 'em all. But the next thing I knew, she was married to a brute called Green."

"Oh, Edward, my dear!" Vera's hand went up to his face, stroking, caressing. The suppressed misery of his voice was almost more than she could bear. "How you suffered!"

He was silent for a moment or two, controlling himself.

"It's over now. Thank God, it's a long time over! She died—less than a year after—when Jack and Robin were born. I'm sorry—I'm very sorry—I hadn't the decency to tell you before we married."

"You needn't be sorry, dear," she said very gently.

He looked at her.

"Do you mean that, Vera? Do you mean it makes no difference to you?"

"No, I don't mean that. I mean that I'm glad nothing happened to ... to prevent my marrying you. I mean ... that I love you ten times more for telling me now."

Thereafter they sat and talked in the firelight for a long time, closely, intimately, as friends united after a long separation. And in that talk the last barrier between them crumbled away, and a bond that was very sacred took its place.

*   *   *

Juliet and Columbus sat in a sheltered nook on the shore and gazed thoughtfully out to sea. It was a warm morning after a night of tempest, and the beach was strewn with seaweed after an unusually high tide.

Suddenly Columbus turned his head sharply. Juliet looked round and in a moment started to her feet. A man's figure, lithe and spare, was coming to her over the stones.

"Oh, Charles!" she said impulsively. "It is good of you to come!"

He glanced round him as he clasped her hand, his face brimming with mischief.

"It is, rather—considering the risk I run. I trust your irascible husband is well out of the way!"

She laughed, though not very heartily.

"Yes, he has gone to town. I didn't want him to. I wish I had stopped him. He has gone up today to see . . . Ivor Yardley."

"What ho!" said Lord Saltash. "This is interesting. And what does he hope to get out of him?"

"I don't know. I had no idea who he was going to see till yesterday evening. Mr. Ashcott came in and they were talking and the name came out."

"And so you sent me an SOS! I am indeed honoured."

She turned towards him, very winningly, very appealingly.

"Charles Rex, I sent for you because I want a friend . . . so very badly. My happiness is in the balance. Don't you understand?"

Her deep voice throbbed with feeling. He stretched out a hand to her with a quick, responsive gesture that somehow belied the imp of mischief in his eyes.

"*Bien, ma Juliette!* I am here!"

"Thank you," she said very earnestly. "I knew I could count on you . . . that you would not withdraw your protection when once you had offered it."

"Would you like my advice as well?" he questioned.

She met his quizzing look with her frank eyes.

"What is your advice?"

He held her hand in his.

"You haven't forgotten, have you, the sole condition on which I extended my protection to you? No, I thought not. We won't discuss it. The time is not yet ripe.

"And as you say, *The Night Moth* in this weather,

though safe, might not be a very comfortable abiding-place. But don't forget she is quite safe, my *Juliette!* I should like you to remember that."

He spoke with a strange emphasis that must in some fashion have conveyed more than his actual words, for quite suddenly her throat worked with a sharp spasm of emotion. She put up her hand instinctively to hide it.

"Thank you," she said. "If I need . . . a city of refuge . . . I shall know which way to turn. Now, for your advice!"

"My advice!"

He was looking at her with those odd, unstable eyes of his that ever barred the way to his inner being.

"It depends a little on the condition of your heart—that. When it comes to this in an obstacle race, there are three courses open to you."

He paused.

"Either you refuse the jump and drop out, which is usually the safest thing to do.

"Or you take the thing at full gallop and clear it before you know where you are.

"Or you go at it with a weak heart and come to grief. I don't advise the last, anyway. It's so futile—as well as being beastly humiliating."

She smiled at him.

"Thank you, Charles! A very illuminating parable! Well, I don't contemplate the first . . . as you know. I must have a try at the second. And if I smash . . . it's horribly difficult, you know . . . I may smash . . ."

Sudden anguish looked at him out of her eyes, and a hard shiver went through her as she turned away.

"Oh, Charles! Why did I ever come to this place?"

He made a frightful grimace that was somehow sympathetic and shrugged his shoulders.

"If you smash, my dearly beloved, your faithful comrade will have the priceless privilege of picking up the pieces. Why you came here is another matter."

His eyes dwelt upon her with a sort of humorous tenderness; she met them without embarrassment.

"You've done me good, Charles. Somehow I knew you would . . . knew I could count on you. You will go on standing by?"

He executed a deep bow, his hand upon his heart.

"*Maintenant et toujours, ma Juliette!*" he assured her gallantly. "But don't forget the moral of my parable! When you jump—jump high!"

She nodded thoughtfully.

"No, I shan't forget. You're a good friend, Charles Rex."

"I may be," replied Lord Saltash enigmatically.

*   *   *

Juliet lunched at the Court in Dick's absence. They thought her somewhat graver and quieter than usual, but there was a gentle aloofness about her that checked all intimate enquiry.

"You are not feeling anxious about the miners?" Vera asked her once.

To which Juliet replied:

"Oh, no! Not in the least; Dick has such a wonderful influence over the men. They would never do any brawling with him there."

"He has no business to drag you into it, all the same," added the Squire.

"They have some cause for grievance," she urged. "At least Dick thinks so."

"Oh, Dick!" replied the Squire. "He'd reform the world if he could. But he's wasting his time. They won't be satisfied till they've had their fling. Lord Wilchester is a wise man to keep out of the way till it's over."

"I'm afraid I don't agree with you there," Juliet said, flushing a little. "He might at least hear what they have to say. But they can't get hold of him. He is abroad."

"But Yardley is left. I suppose he has powers to act."

"Perhaps," she replied, the moment's animation passing. "But it is Wilchester's business . . . not his. He shirks his duty."

"I notice you never have a good word for any of the Farringmore family," said the Squire quizzically, with a half-smile on his face.

She shook her head.

"They are all so selfish. It's the family failing, I'm afraid."

"You don't share, it, anyhow," said Vera.

"Ah! You don't know me," replied Juliet.

They went for a long motor-ride when the meal was over, but at the end of it, it seemed to Vera that they had talked solely of her affairs throughout.

They had tea on their return, but Juliet would not stay any later. She must be back, she said, to meet Dick and be sure that the supper was ready in good time.

As for Juliet, she hastened away as one in a fever to escape, yet before she reached the end of the avenue her feet moved as if weighted with chains.

Dick had not returned, and she went into the little Dining-Room and busied herself with laying the cloth for supper.

She could hear Mrs. Rickett, who often came up to help, moving about the kitchen. She did not feel in the mood for the good woman's chatter, and delayed going in her direction as long as possible.

So it came about that, pausing for a few moments at the window before doing so, she heard the click of the gate and saw the old postman coming up the path.

"Evening, Ma'am! Here's a parcel for you!" the old man said. "It's books, and it's all come to bits, but I don't think as I've dropped any of 'em."

The parcel was certainly badly damaged, and books in white covers began to slide out of it the moment they were released.

"I'll leave you to sort 'em, Ma'am," he said airily. "Well, I'll be getting along to the Court, Ma'am, and I wish you a very good night."

He stamped away, and in the failing evening light Juliet began to gather up the confusion he had left behind.

She found it was not a collection of paperback school-books, as she had at first imagined, and since the contents of the parcel were very thoroughly scattered she glanced at them with idle curiosity as she laid them together.

Then with a sudden violent start she picked up one of the volumes and looked at it closely. The title stood out with arresting clearness on the white paper jacket: *Gold of the Desert*, by Dene Strange, author of *The Valley of Dry Bones, Marionettes*, etc.

Her heart was beating so fast that it seemed continuous, like the dull roar of the sea. The volumes were all alike, all copies of one book.

A sheet of paper fluttered from the one she held.

Author's Copies—With Compliments were the words that stood out before her widening gaze. She remained as one transfixed, staring at them. It was as if a thunderbolt had fallen in the quiet room. . . .

And then, very suddenly, she was on her feet, tense, palpitating, her head turned to listen. The gate had clicked again, and someone was coming up the path.

It was Dick, moving with the step of an eager man as he reached the door, opened it, and entered. She heard him in the passage, heard his tread upon the threshold, heard his voice greeting her.

"Hullo, darling! All alone in the dark? I've had a beast of a day away from you."

His hands reached out and clasped her. She was actually in his arms before she found her voice.

"Dick! Dick! Please! I want to speak to you."

He clasped her close. His lips pressed hers, stopping all utterance for a while with a mastery that would not be held in check. She could not resist him, but there was no rapture in her yielding.

Suddenly, with his face against her neck, he spoke.

"What's the matter, Juliet?"

She quivered in response, made an attempt to release herself, felt his arms tighten, and was still.

"I have found out something," she said, her voice very low.

"What is it?"

She did not answer. A great impulse arose in her to wrench herself from him, to thrust him back; but she could not. She stood, a prisoner, in his arms.

He waited a moment, still with his face bent over her, his lips close to her neck.

"Is it anything that—matters?"

She felt his arms drawing her and quivered again like a trapped bird.

"Yes," she whispered.

"Very much?"

"Yes," she said again.

"Then you are angry with me?"

She was silent.

He pressed her suddenly very close.

"Juliet, you don't hate me, do you?"

She caught her breath with a sob that sounded painfully hard and dry.

"I couldn't have married you . . . if I had known."

He started a little and lifted his head.

"As bad as that!" he said.

For a space there was silence between them while his eyes dwelt sombrely upon the litter of books upon the table, and still his arms enfolded her, though he did not hold her close.

When at last she made as if she would release herself, he still would not let her go.

"Will you listen to me?" he asked. "Give me a hearing—just for a minute? You have forgiven so much in me that is really bad that I can't feel this last to be—quite unpardonable."

He hesitated, then went on:

"Juliet, I haven't really wronged you. You have got a false impression of the man who wrote those books. Will you defer judgement—for my sake—till you have read this latest book, written when you first came into my life?

"Will you—Juliet, will you have patience till I have proved myself?"

She shivered as she stood.

"You don't know . . . what you have done."

He made a quick gesture of protest.

"Yes, I do know. I know quite well. I have hurt you, deceived you. But hear my defence, anyway!

"I never meant to marry you in the first place without telling you, but I always wanted you to read this book of mine first. It's different from the others, and I wanted you to see the difference."

He paused for a moment.

"I waited till the book could be published and you could read it. I wanted you—so badly—to read it with an open mind. And now, whichever way you look at it, you certainly won't do that."

There was a whimsical note in his voice, despite its obvious sincerity, as he ended, and Juliet winced as she heard it, and in a moment with resolution freed herself from his hold.

She did it in silence, but there was that in the action that deeply wounded him. He stood motionless, looking at her, a glitter of sternness in his eyes.

"Juliet," he said after a moment, "you are not treating this matter reasonably. I admit I tricked you, but my love for you was my excuse. And those books of mine were never intended for such as you."

She looked at him with a kind of frozen wonder.

"Then who were they meant for?"

He made a slight movement of impatience.

"You know. You know very well. They were meant for the people whom you yourself despise, the crowd you broke away from—men and women like the Farringmores who live for nothing but their own pleasure."

She went back against the table and stood there, supporting herself while she still faced him.

"You forget," she said, her voice very low, "I think you forget . . . that they are my people . . . I belong to them!"

"No, you don't!" he flung back almost fiercely. "You belong to me!"

A great shiver went through her. She clenched her hands to repress it.

"I don't see," she said, "how I can possibly stay with you after this."

"What?"

He strode forward and caught her by the shoulders. She was aware of a sudden hot blaze of anger in him. He held her in a grip that was merciless.

"Do you know what you are saying?" he asked.

She bowed her head against his shoulder.

"Oh, Dick! It is you who don't know!"

"And so you think you can leave me—as lightly as Lady Joanna Farringmore left that man I went to see today?"

She lifted her head with a gasp.

"No! Oh, no! Not . . . like that!"

His eyes pierced her with their appalling brightness.

"No, not quite like that," he retorted, with awful grimness. "There is a difference. An engaged woman can cut the cable and be free without assistance. A married woman needs a lover to help her!"

She shrank afresh from the scorching cynicism of his words.

"Dick! Have I asked for freedom?"

"You had better not ask," he flashed back. "You have gone too far already. I tell you, Juliet, when you gave yourself to me it was irrevocable. There's no going back now. You have got to put up with me—whatever the cost."

"Ah!" she whispered.

"Listen! This thing is going to make no difference between us—no difference whatever. You cared for me enough to marry me, and I am the same man now that I was then. And if you leave me—well, I shall follow you and bring you back."

His lips closed implacably upon the words; he held her as though challenging her to free herself. But Juliet neither moved nor spoke. She stood absolutely passive in his hold, waiting in utter silence.

He stood for a moment longer, then abruptly his hold tightened upon her. She lifted her face then sharply, resisting him almost instinctively, and in that instant his passion burst its bonds.

He crushed her to him with sudden mastery, and so, compelling, he kissed her hotly, possessively, dominatingly, holding her lips with his own, till she strained against him no longer, but hung, burning and quivering, at his mercy.

Then at length, very slowly, he released her. She leant upon the table, trembling, her hands covering her face. And he stood behind her, breathing heavily, saying no word.

She stirred and rose unsteadily. He put out a hand to help her. She did not take it, indeed she did not seem even to see it.

Gropingly, she turned to the door, went out slowly, still as if feeling her way, reached the narrow stairs, and went up them, clutching at the rail.

When Mrs. Rickett entered with a lamp a few moments later, he was gathering up the litter of books and paper from the table, his face white and sternly set. He gave her a brief word of greeting, and went across to the school with his burden.

Chapter
Eight

It was a dumb and sullen crowd that Dick Green faced that night in the great barn on the slope of High Shale.

Dick, entering at the door at the platform end of the building instead of passing straight up through the crowd as was his custom, was aware of a curious influence at work from the first moment, an influence adverse if not directly hostile that reached him he knew not how.

He heard a vague murmur as Juliet and Lord Saltash followed him, and sharply he turned and drew Juliet to his side. In that instant he realised that she was the only woman in the place.

He faced the crowd, his hand upon her arm.

"Well, men," he said, his words clean-cut and ready, "so you've left your wives behind, have you? I, on the contrary, have brought mine, and she has promised to give you a song."

The mutter died. Some youths at the back started applause, which spread though somewhat half-heartedly through the crowd, and for a space the ugly feeling died down.

"Are you ready?" he said to Juliet.

She rose and came forward, tall and graceful, bearing the unmistakable stamp of breeding in every delicate movement. She might have been on the platform of a London concert-hall as she faced her audience under the shadowing hat.

They stared at her open-mouthed, spellbound, awed

by the quiet dignity of her. And in the hush that fell
before her, Juliet began to sing.

Her voice was low, highly trained, exquisitely soft.
She sang an old English ballad with a throbbing sweetness
that held her audience with its charm. And behind her
Dick softly accompanied her on his banjo.

His face was in shadow also as he bent over the
instrument. Not once throughout the song did he look
up.

When she ended, there came that involuntary pause
which is the highest tribute that can be paid by any
audience, and then such a thunder of applause as shook
the building.

And Juliet sang again and again, thrilling the rough
crowd as Dick had never thrilled them, choosing such
old-world melodies as reach the hearts of all.

The whole atmosphere of the place had altered. The
heavy sullenness had passed like a thunder-cloud, and
Ashcott was no longer smoking his pipe in the doorway
with an air of gloomy foreboding.

Dick laid aside his banjo and came to the front of the
platform. There was absolute confidence in his bearing, a
vital strength that imparted a mastery that yet was largely
compounded of comradeship.

He began to speak without effort, as a man spoke to
his friends.

It was at this point that Ashcott touched him on the
shoulder with a muttered word that made him turn
sharply.

"What? Who?"

"Mr. Ivor Yardley!" the manager muttered uneasily.
"He's waiting to speak to you—says he'll address the men
if you'll allow him."

Juliet's look followed his. She stood up quickly.

"Dick! Who is it?"

Something in her voice brought his eyes back to her
in sudden close scrutiny.

For that instant he forgot the crowd of men and the
need of the moment, forgot the man who waited in the
background whom he had desired so urgently to see,
forgot the whole world in the wide-eyed terror of her
look.

Instinctively he stretched an arm behind her, but in

the same moment Lord Saltash came swiftly forward to
her other side, and it was Lord Saltash who spoke with
the quick, intimate reassurance of the trusted friend.

"It's all right, *Juliette*. I'm here to take care of you.
Give them one more song, won't you? Afterwards, if
you've had enough of it, I'll take you back."

She turned her face towards him and away from
Dick, whose arm fell from her unheeded; but her gaze did
not leave the leather-clad figure that stood waiting in the
dim doorway, upright, grim as Fate.

"Don't be afraid!" urged Lord Saltash in his rapid
whisper. "Anyhow, don't show it! I'll see you through."

She made a blind gesture towards him and in an
instant his hand gripped her elbow.

"Can't you do it? Are you going to drop out?"

She recovered herself sharply, as though something
in his words had pierced her pride. The next moment very
quietly she turned back to Dick.

"I am quite ready," she said.

He took her hand without a word and led her
forward. Someone raised a cheer for her and in a second a
shout of applause thundered to the rafters.

Dick smiled a brief smile of gratitude and lifted a
hand for silence. Then, as it fell, he stepped back.

And Juliet stood alone before the rough crowd.

Those who saw her in that moment never forgot her.
Tall and slender, she stood and faced the men below her.
But no song rose to her lips, and those who were nearest
to her thought that she was trembling.

Then suddenly she began to speak in a full, quiet
voice that penetrated the deep hush with a bell-like
clearness.

"Men," she said, "it is very kind of you to cheer me,
but you will never do it again. I have something to tell
you. I don't know in the least how you will take it, but I
hope you will manage to forgive me if you possibly
can.

"Mr. Green is your friend, and he knows nothing
about it, so you will acquit him of all blame.

"I know you all hate the Farringmores, and I daresay
you have reason. You have never spoken to any of them
face to face, before, because they haven't cared enough to
come near you. But ... you can do so tonight if you
wish.

"Men, I am ... Lord Wilchester's sister. I was ... Joanna Farringmore."

She ceased to speak, with a little gesture of the hands that was quite involuntary and oddly pathetic, but she did not turn away from her audience.

Throughout the deep silence that followed that amazing confession she stood quite straight and still, waiting, her face to the throng.

A hoarse murmur broke out at the back of the great barn, spreading like a wave on the sea. Lord Saltash's hand closed upon Juliet's arm, drawing her back with gentle firmness.

As Lord Saltash led her to the back of the platform she had a glimpse of Dick's face, white as death, with lips hard-set and stern as she had never seen them, and a glitter in his eyes that made her think of onyx.

He passed her by without a glance. The man in the leather coat was with him. He paused before Juliet, a cynical smile playing about his face. It was a face of iron mastery, of pitiless self-assertion. The eyes were as points of steel.

He bent towards her and spoke.

"I thought I should find you sooner or later, Lady Jo. I trust you have enjoyed your game—even if you have lost your winnings!"

And Yardley laughed, an edged laugh that was inexpressibly cruel.

Lord Saltash's arm went round Juliet like a coiled spring. He impelled her, unresisting, to the door. Her hand rested on his shoulder as she stepped down from the platform. She went with him as one in a dream.

Lord Saltash hurried her up the slope to the place where he had left his car. It stood at the side of the rough road that led to High Shale Point.

"Get in!" he ordered.

She obeyed, sinking down with a vague thankfulness, conscious of great weakness.

But as he cranked the engine and she felt the throb of movement she sat up quickly.

"Charles, what am I doing? Where are you taking me?"

He came round to her and his hands clasped hers for a moment in a grip that was warm and close. He did not speak at once.

Then he said lightly:

"I don't know what you'll do afterwards, *ma Juliette*. But you are coming with me now!"

She caught her breath as if she would utter some protest, but something checked her, perhaps it was the memory of Dick's face as she had last seen it, stony, grimly averted, uncompromisingly stern.

She gripped his hands in answer, but she did not speak a word.

And so they sped away together into the dark.

* * *

It was very late that night, and the sea mist had turned to a drifting rain, when the Squire, sitting reading in his Library at the Court, was startled by a sudden tapping upon the window behind him.

So unexpected was the sound in the absolute stillness that he started with some violence. Then, sharply and frowning, he arose. He reached the window and peered through the glass.

"Who is it? What do you want?"

A face he knew, but so drawn and deathly that for the moment it seemed almost unfamiliar, peered back at him. In a second he had the window unfastened and flung wide.

"Dick! In heaven's name, boy, what's the matter?"

Dick was over the sill in a single bound. He stood and faced the Squire, bare-headed, drenched with rain, his eyes burning with a terrible fire.

"I have come for my wife," he said.

"Your wife! Juliet!" The Squire stared at him as if he thought him demented. "Why, she left ages ago, man—soon after tea!"

"Yes, yes, I know," Dick answered. He spoke rapidly but with decision. "But she came back here an hour or two ago. You are giving her shelter. Lord Saltash brought her, or no, she probably came alone."

"You are mad!" replied the Squire, and turned to shut the window. "She hasn't been near since she left this evening."

"Wait!" Dick's hand shot out and caught his arm, restraining him. "Do you swear to me that you don't know where she is?"

The Squire stood still, looking full and hard into the

face so near his own; and he realised what he had not grasped before—that it was the face of a man in torture.

The savage grip on his arm told the same story. The fiery eyes that stared at him out of the death-white countenance had the awful look of a man who sees his last hope shattered.

Impulsively he laid his free hand upon him.

"Dick, Dick old chap—what's all this? Of course I don't know where she is! Do you think I'd lie to you?"

"Then I've lost her!" Dick said, and with the words some vital inner spring seemed to snap within him. He flung up his arms, freeing himself with a wild gesture. "My God, she has gone—gone with that scoundrel!"

"Saltash?" said the Squire sharply.

"Yes. Saltash!" He ground the name between his teeth. "Does that surprise you so very much? Don't you know the sort of infernal blackguard he is?"

The Squire turned again to shut the window.

"Damn it, Dick! I don't believe a word of it."

Dick drew a deep breath.

"You'll think I'm mad, Sir. I thought I was myself at first. But it's true—it must be true. I heard it from her own lips. Juliet—my wife—my wife—is—was—Lady Joanna Farringmore!"

"Great heavens!" said the Squire. "Dick, are you sure?"

"Yes, quite sure. She was caught—caught by Yardley at the meeting tonight. She couldn't escape, so she told the truth—told the whole crowd—and then bolted—bolted with Saltash."

"Great heavens! But what was Saltash doing there?"

"Oh, he came to protect her. He knew, or guessed, that there was something in the wind. He came to support her. I know now. He's the subtlest devil that ever was made."

"But why on earth—why on earth did she ever come here?" questioned the Squire.

"She was hiding from Yardley, of course. He's a cold, vindictive brute, and I suppose—I suppose she was afraid of him, and came to me—came to me—for refuge."

Dick was speaking through his hands.

"That's how he regards it himself. She was always playing fast and loose till she got engaged to him. But he—I imagine no-one ever played with him before. He swears—swears he'll make her suffer for it yet."

"Pooh!" retorted the Squire. "How does he propose to do that? She's your wife anyhow."

"My wife—yes." Slowly Dick raised his head, stared for a space in front of him, then grimly rose. "My wife—as you say, Sir. And I'm going to find her—now."

"I'm coming with you."

"No, Sir, no!" Dick looked at him with a tight-lipped smile that was somehow terrible. "Don't do that! You won't want to be a witness against me."

"Pooh!" said the Squire again. "I may be of use to you before it comes to that. But before we start, let me tell you one thing, Dick! She married you because she loves you—for no other reason."

A sharp spasm contracted Dick's hard features; he set his lips and said nothing.

"She loves you," the Squire went on, "Lady Jo—or no Lady Jo—she loves you. It wasn't make-believe. She's run away from you now—run away with another man because she couldn't stay and face you. Is she afraid of you then?"

Dick threw up his head with the action of a goaded animal.

"Yes."

"Then you've given her some reason?"

"Yes. I have given her reason!"

Fiercely he flung the words.

"This evening she found out something about me which even you don't know yet—something that made her hate me. She said if she had known of it she would never have married me."

Dick spoke with intense bitterness.

"I didn't realise then—how could I?—how hard it hit her. And I made her understand that, having married me, it was irrevocable. That was why she ran away with Saltash. She didn't trust me any longer."

"But, my dear fellow, what in heaven's name is this awful thing that even I don't know?" demanded the Squire. "Don't tell me there has ever been any damn trouble with another woman?"

"During the past few years some books have been published by one named Dene Strange that have attracted attention in certain quarters."

"I've read 'em all," said the Squire. "Well?"

"I wrote them—that's all."

"You!" the Squire stared. "You, Dick!"

"Yes, I. And then—when she came—she told me she hated the man who wrote those books for being cynical and merciless.

"So I wrote another to make her change her mind about me before she knew. It is only just published. And she found out before she read it.

"That's all," Dick said again, with the shadow of a smile. "She found out this evening."

He paused, stood a moment as if bracing himself, then turned.

"Well, I'm going, Sir. Come if you really must, but I don't advise it."

"I am coming," said the Squire briefly.

His hand went from Dick's shoulder to his arm and gave it a hard squeeze.

"Confound you! What do you take me for?"

Dick's hand came swiftly to his.

"I take you for the best friend a man ever had, Sir."

"Pooh!" said the Squire.

*　*　*

Ten minutes later they went down the dripping avenue in the Squire's little car. The drifting fog made an inky blackness of the night, and progress was very slow under the trees.

The light at the lodge gates flung a wide glare through the mist, and he steered for it with more assurance. They passed through and turned into the road.

And here the Squire pulled up with a jerk, for immediately in front of them another light shone.

"What the devil is that, Dick?"

"It's another car," said Dick, and jumped out. "Hullo, there! Anything the matter?"

"Damnation, yes!" answered a voice. "I've run into this infernal wall and damaged my radiator."

"Who is it?" said Dick sharply.

He was standing almost touching the car, but he could not see the speaker.

A sound that was curiously like a chuckle answered him out of the darkness, but no reply came in words.

Dick stood motionless.

"Saltash!" he said incredulously. "Is it Saltash?"

"Why shouldn't it be Saltash?" said a voice that laughed. "That you, Romeo? Afraid I've knocked a few chips off your beastly wall. What are you keeping so quiet about? Aren't you pleased to see me? Not that you can—but that's a detail."

Dick spoke with deadly quietness through lips that did not seem to move.

"Where have you taken my wife?"

"Oh, she's quite safe," replied Lord Saltash, and smiled with a flash of teeth. "I am taking every care of her. You need have no anxiety about that."

"I asked where you had taken her," Dick said, his words low and distinct, wholly without emotion.

Lord Saltash's eyes began to gleam.

"I heard you, *mon ami*. But since the lady is under my protection at the present moment, I am not prepared to answer that question off-hand. When I give my protection to anyone—I give it."

"Is that what you came back to say?" asked Dick, still without stirring hand or feature.

"By no means. I didn't come to see you at all. I came to fetch Columbus!"

Something that was like an electric thrill went through Dick. He took a sudden step forward.

"Damn you!" he said, and gripped Lord Saltash by the collar. "Tell me where she is! Do you hear? Tell me!"

Lord Saltash straightened himself with a lightning movement. They looked into each other's eyes for several tense seconds. Then, though no word had passed between them, Dick's hand fell.

"That's better," Lord Saltash said. "You're getting quite civil. Look here, my bully-boy! I'll tell you something, and you'd better listen carefully, for there's a hidden meaning to it. You're the biggest ass that ever trod this earth. There!"

He put up a hand to his crumpled collar and straighten it, still with his eyes upon Dick's face.

"Got that?" he asked abruptly. "Well then I'll tell you something else. I've got a revolver in my pocket. But you shall have it to shoot me with, if you will answer honestly one question I should like to put to you first. Is it a deal?"

Dick was breathing quickly. He stood close to Lord Saltash, urged by a deadly enmity and still on the verge of violence, but restrained by something about the other man's attitude that he could not have defined.

"Well?" he said curtly at length. "What do you want to know?"

Lord Saltash's lips twisted in a faintly sardonic smile.

"Just one thing. If some kind friend had come to you, say, the night before your wedding and told you that you were about to marry Lady Jo Farringmore, would you have gone ahead with it—or not?"

Dick's eyes blazed.

"Of course I should have married her!"

"You are sure of that?"

"Damn you—yes!" With terrific force Dick answered him.

Lord Saltash held out a revolver to Dick on the palm of his hand.

"Here you are! It's fully loaded. If you want to shoot a friend, you'll never have a better chance."

Dead silence followed his words. Dick's face threw into strong relief every set, grim feature. His lips were tightly compressed, a single straight line across his stern face. His eyes never varied; they were almost unbearably bright.

They held Lord Saltash's with a tensity of purpose that was greater than any display of physical force. It was as if the two were locked in silent combat.

Then, very steadily, without a word Dick held out his hand.

Lord Saltash's came to meet it. They looked each other again in the eyes, but with a difference. Then Lord Saltash began to laugh.

"Go to her, my cavalier! You'll find her waiting on *The Night Moth*."

"Waiting?" Dick said.

"For Columbus," replied Lord Saltash with his most derisive grin, and tossed Dick's hand away.

* * *

A chill breeze sprang up in the dark of the early morning and blew the drifting fog away. The stars came out one by one till the whole sky shone and quivered as if it had been pricked by a million glittering spear-points.

And in the state cabin of *The Night Moth*, the woman who had knelt for hours by the velvet couch lifted her face to the open port-hole and shivered.

Her face was dead white, drawn with unspeakable weariness, with the piteous lines about the eyes that only long watching can bring. She looked hopeless, beaten.

The cold air blew round her, and again she shivered as one chilled to the heart, but she made no move to pick up the cloak that had fallen from her shoulders.

And then suddenly out of the utter quietness there came a sound, the scuttle of scampering feet and an eager whining at the door behind her. It stabbed like a needle through her lethargy. In a moment she was on her feet.

The door burst in upon her as she opened it, and immediately she was sprung upon and almost borne backwards by the wriggling, ecstatic figure of Columbus. He flung himself into her arms with yelps of extravagant joy.

It took some time for his rapturous greetings to subside, but finally he dropped upon the couch beside her, pressed to her, temporarily exhausted, but still wriggling spasmodically whenever her hand moved upon him.

And then Juliet, for some odd reason that she could not have explained, found herself crying in the darkness as she had not cried all through that night of anguish.

It was Columbus who told her by a sudden change of attitude that someone had entered at the open door and was standing close to her in the dark.

She started upright very swiftly as the dog jumped down to welcome the intruder. Vaguely through the dimness she saw a figure and leapt to her feet, her hands tight-clasped upon her racing heart.

"Charles! Why have you come here?"

There was an instant of stillness, then a swift movement and a man's arms caught her as she stood and she was a prisoner.

She made a wild struggle for freedom.

"No . . . no!" she panted. "Let me go!"

But he held her fast, so fast that she gasped and gasped for breath, saying no word, only holding her, till suddenly she cried out sharply and her resistance broke.

She hid her face against him.

"You!" she breathed. "You!"

He held her yet in silence for a space, and through the silence she heard the beat of his heart, quick and hard, as if he had been running a race.

Then over her bowed head he spoke, his voice deep, vibrant, seeming to hold back some inner leaping force.

"Didn't I tell you I should follow you and bring you back?"

She shrank at his words.

"I can't come . . . I can't come!"

"You will come, Juliet."

"No . . . no!" She lifted her head in sudden passionate protest. "Not to be tortured! I can't face it! Before God I would rather . . . I would rather die!"

"And don't you think I would rather die than let you go?"

"Ah!" she said, and no more, for the fierce possession of his hold checked all remonstrance.

Again a great tremor went through her. She bent her head a little lower to hide her tears. But they fell upon his hands and she could not check them. She became suddenly blinded and overwhelmed by bitter weeping.

"Ah, Juliet—Juliet!" he said, and went down on his knees before her, holding her closely, closely to his breast. . . .

It seemed to her a very long time later that she found herself lying exhausted against the sofa-cushions, feeling his arm still about her and poignantly conscious of his touch.

She could not remember that he had spoken a single word since he had taken her into his arms, neither had he kissed her, but all her fear of him was gone.

Moved by a deep impulse, she took the hand that lay upon her brow and drew it downwards to her lips, then softly to her heart, while she turned her eyes to his.

"Oh, Dick, are you sure . . . are you quite sure . . . that . . . that . . . I am worth keeping?"

"I am quite sure I am going to keep you," he answered.

Her two hands closed fast upon his.

"Not . . . not as a prisoner?" she whispered, wanly smiling.

"Yes, a prisoner," he said, not without a certain grimness; "that is, until you have learnt your lesson."

"What lesson?" she asked him wonderingly.

"That you can't do without me," he answered, a note of challenge in his voice.

Something in his look hurt her. She freed one hand and laid it pleadingly, caressingly, against his neck.

"Oh, Dicky, try to understand!"

His face changed a little, and she thought his mouth quivered ever so slightly as he said:

"It's now or never, Juliet. If I don't come to a perfect understanding with you tonight, we shall be strangers for the rest of our lives."

She shivered at the finality of his words, but they gave her light.

"I have hurt you horribly," she said.

He was silent.

She pressed herself to him with a sudden passionate gesture.

"Dick . . . my husband . . . will you forgive me . . . can you forgive me . . . before you understand?"

Her eyes implored him, yet just for a second he hesitated. Then very swiftly he gathered her closely, closely against his heart, and kissed her pleading, up-turned face over and over.

"Yes! Yes!" he said.

She clung to him with all her quivering strength.

"I love you, darling! I love you . . . only . . . only . . . you!" she whispered brokenly. "You believe that?"

"Yes," he said again between kisses.

"And then . . . and then . . . I had such an awful doubt of you, Dicky. I thought your love was dead, and I thought . . . and I thought I couldn't hope to hold you . . . after that. I'd got to free you somehow. Oh, Dicky, what agony love can be!"

"Hush, darling, hush!"

She lay in his arms, her eyes looking straight up to his.

"Dicky, listen! I've had a horrid life. My mother was divorced when Muff and I were youngsters at school. My father died only a year after, and no-one ever cared what happened to us after that."

She paused, for Dick's arms had tightened about her.

"I just went with the crowd and pleased myself. Sometimes I hurt people but I didn't care."

"That doesn't sound like you."

"That was me," she returned, with a touch of recklessness, "till I read that first book of yours, *The Valley of Dry Bones*. That brought me up short. It shocked me horribly. You cut very deep, Dicky. I'm carrying the scars still."

He bent without words and set his lips to her forehead, keeping them there in mute caress while she went on:

"I had just begun to play with Ivor Yardley. He was my latest catch, and I was rather proud of him. And then, after reading that book, I felt so evil, so unspeakably ashamed, that, when I knew he was really in earnest, I accepted him."

She shuddered suddenly and twined her arm about her husband's neck.

"Dicky, I went through hell after that. I tried . . . I tried very hard to be honourable . . . to keep my word. But when the time drew near I simply couldn't. And so, almost at the last moment I let him down . . . I ran away."

She paused.

"And oh, Dicky, the peace of this place after all that misery and turmoil! It was heaven. And I thought . . . I thought it was going to be quite easy to be good!"

"And then I came and upset it all," murmured Dick, with his lips against her hair.

Her hold tightened.

"It's been one perpetual struggle against appalling odds ever since," she said. "If it hadn't been for Robin I should never have married you."

"Yes, you would," he replied quietly. "That was meant. I've realised that since."

"I'm not sure. If you hadn't been so miserable I should have told you the truth. You wouldn't have married me then."

"Yes, I should."

She drew a little away to look into his face.

"Dick, are you sure of that?"

"I am quite sure. It's just because I am sure that I am with you now—instead of Lord Saltash. It was his own test."

Her eyes met his unflinchingly.

"Dick, you believe that Charles and I are just friends?"

"I believe it."

"And you are not angry with him?"

"No." He spoke with slight effort. "I am grateful to him."

"But you don't like him?"

He hesitated momentarily.

"Do you?"

"Yes, of course." Her brows contracted a little. "I can't help it. I always have."

He bent abruptly and kissed them.

"All right, darling. So do I."

She smiled at him, clinging closely.

"Dicky, that's the most generous thing you ever did!"

"Oh, I can afford to be generous," he answered, "now that I know your secrets and you know mine. Will you tell me something else now, Juliet?"

"Yes, darling," she whispered.

He laid his cheek against hers.

"I was going to tell you my secret when you had read that last book of mine. When were you going to tell me yours?"

"Oh, Dicky!" she said in some confusion, and hid her face against his neck.

"No, tell me! I want to know."

But Juliet only clung a little faster to him and buried her face a little deeper.

"Weren't you ever going to tell me?" he questioned.

"Oh yes . . . sometime," she murmured from his breast.

"Well, when?" he persisted. "Just anytime?"

"No, dear, of course not!" A muffled sound that was half-sob and half-laugh came with the words.

Dick waited for a space, and then very gently began to feel for the hidden face. She tried to resist him; then, finding he would not be resisted, she took his hand and pressed it over her eyes, holding it as a shield between them.

"Won't you tell me?" he asked.

She trembled a little in his hold.

"That . . . that . . . is another secret, Dicky," she said very softly.

"Mayn't I share it, sweetheart?"

She uncovered her eyes with a little tremulous laugh, and lifted them to his.

"Oh, I'm a coward, Dicky, a horrid coward. I thought
. . . I thought I would tell you everything when . . . when
you were holding your son in your arms. I thought you
would have to forgive me then."

"Oh, Juliet—Juliet!"

He tried to smile in answer but could not. His lips
quivered suddenly and he laid his head down upon her
breast.

And so, with her arms round him and the warm
throbbing of her heart against his face, he came to the
perfect understanding.

They saw the morning break through a silver mist,
standing side-by-side on deck with the water sweeping
snow-white from their keel.

Juliet, within the circle of her husband's arm, looked
up and broke the silence with a sigh and a smile.

"Good-morning, Romeo! And now that I've learnt my
lesson, hadn't we better be going home?"

He kissed her and drew her cloak more closely round
her.

"Do you want to go home?" he asked.

She looked at him with a whimsical frown.

"Well, I think I am at home wherever you are. But
you are such a busy man. You can't be spared."

"They've got to spare me for today."

"Ah! And tomorrow?"

"Tomorrow too. Juliet, I'm giving up my work at
Little Shale."

"But you can't give it up at a moment's notice."

"The Squire is managing it. By the way, Juliet, I've a
piece of news for you. You know what Yardley came
for?"

"No, I don't," she said, looking momentarily startled.

His hand reassured her.

"No, not for you, darling. He didn't expect to find
you. No, he came because he had been told that I was
doing the work of an agitator among the men."

"Dick!" She spoke with quick indignation. "How dare
he?"

His touch restrained her.

"It doesn't matter. He came to see for himself, and he
knows better now. He told me after the meeting that I
could take over his share of the concern if I liked.

"And I took him at his word then and there. I've got

some money put by, and the Squire can put up the rest. Do you think your brother will mind?"

"Muff! Oh, no! He never minds anything."

"I'll buy him out too, then, someday, and we'll make that mine a going concern, Juliet. I'll teach those men to use their brains instead of being led by these infernal revolutionists."

Juliet's eyes were shining.

"Bravo, Dick," she said softly.

He met her look.

"You'll have to help me, sweetheart."

She gave him both her hands.

"I will help you in all that you do, Dick."

It was at this point that Columbus, who had been sitting a little apart with his back turned, got up, shook himself vigorously as if to give warning of his approach, and went to Juliet.

He set his paws against her with a loud pathetic yawn.

She bent over him.

"Oh, poor Columbus! He's so bored! Do you want to go home, my Christopher?"

"Poor chap!" said Dick. "It is rather hard to be dragged away on someone else's honeymoon whether you want to or not. Had enough of it, eh? Think it's high time we took the missis home?"

Columbus snuffled into his hand, and wagged himself from the tail upwards.

Juliet put her arms round him and kissed him.

"Dear old fellow, of course he does! He thinks we are just the silliest people alive. Perhaps from some points of view we are."

Columbus said nothing, but he surveyed them both with a look of twinkling humour, and then smothered a laugh with a sneeze.

ABOUT THE EDITOR

BARBARA CARTLAND, the world's most famous romantic novelist, who is also an historian, playwright, lecturer, political speaker and television personality, has now written over 200 books.

She has also had many historical works published and has written four autobiographies as well as the biographies of her mother and that of her brother Ronald Cartland, who was the first Member of Parliament to be killed in the last war. This book has a preface by Sir Winston Churchill.

Barbara Cartland has sold 100 million books over the world, more than half of these in the U.S.A. She broke the world record in 1975 by writing twenty books, and her own record in 1976 with twenty-one. In addition, her album of love songs has just been published, sung with the Royal Philharmonic Orchestra.

In private life, Barbara Cartland, who is a Dame of the Order of St. John of Jerusalem, has fought for better conditions and salaries for Midwives and Nurses. As President of the Royal College of Midwives (Hertfordshire Branch), she has been invested with the first Badge of Office ever given in Great Britain which was subscribed to by the Midwives themselves. She has also championed the cause for old people and founded the first Romany Gypsy Camp in the world.

Barbara Cartland is deeply interested in Vitamin Therapy and is President of the British National Association for Health.